I0657563

I Didn't Want To Be The Karma Killer
(The Karma Killer Saga - Book 1)

By Brandon Nathaniel Boodoosingh

Please be advised, this story contains highly controversial subjects and includes graphic violence, ridiculous and unneeded amounts of crude language, human trafficking, sexual abuse, child abuse, mutilation, and unfortunately, much more.

Be wary or just leave if you are easily triggered or can ever be triggered at all.

Everything included in these stories is probably fictional unless stated otherwise, but I still urge you not to do any deep research on Darklind, or any other mentioned supposedly fictional places.

References and depictions of real people who may be mentioned, alluded to, depicted, or bear any resemblance to anyone in this book and the subsequent books, are entirely fictional, even when completely accurate, factual, and true.

One Bad Day

Look, I didn't want to be a serial killer.

I actually wanted to be a superhero.

But I can't fly by flinging myself across vast
distances, throw around planets to play
catch with my brother, cause the heat death
of the universe with my eyes, push
universes apart with my hands, none of that.

Because superheroes aren't real.

It's a world of wild animals, humans
included.

There are no superhumans.

No one has powers

It's boring…

Being able to fly sounds fun...

But the superhero dream is why I had my
parents change my name to Karma when I
was a kid.

Then things went wrong and I gave up on
my superhero dream, keeping my name as
a reminder of what I had done.

A memento of what I am.

A scar of my past.

And an inevitable truth of how actions work.

A truth that even I can't escape, only run from.

Listen, I don't think I'm a psychopath.

Then again, children can't be diagnosed with psychopathy, but I haven't even been diagnosed with a conduct disorder.

But yeah, I do dress up in an all-black costume and kill people who hurt others.

But I'm not insane.

At least, I'm not insane in a way that would give me any leverage in court.

To rule insanity, I'd have to be undeniably not in control of my actions.

I'm always in control.

But, insane or not, I am a killer.

I don't know when I became whatever I am.

Because I'm not sure what I am.

I just know that I stared into the abyss.

And I jumped in.

My name is Karma, Karma Leto.

I'm 12 years old.

And I'm a serial killer.

…

I was checking out items at a store, a boxcutter, a rope, and some duct tape.

I narrowed my eyes as the man walked away.

I'll admit this once, I was short.

This man was a bit taller.

"I'll make sure you're paid extra boss, I'm leavin' early," I told my manager.

"Sure Karma! Thank you!" She said,

Yes, she thanked me.

I changed out of my work clothes, followed the man to an alley, and hid behind a wall.

I'm so lucky it was fall, a few months later and I'd be freezing.

The man stood for two hours.

I almost just gouged my eyes out just to have something to do.

No, wait, that'd hurt… a lot.

I can function fine with 4 hours of sleep, it helps me game with my overseas companions, this was nothing.

But when gaming, I had games and friends, right now I was just stalking this weirdo.

Then, finally, at a few minutes past 6 in the evening, a woman walked into view, she was noticeably intoxicated despite the time and proceeded to puke on the floor.

The man approached the woman and grabbed her arm.

She stared at the man for a moment.

Then…

"What are you doing? Let go of my arm!" The woman shrieked in a slurred tone.

Of course, people heard, but it was nothing unusual in this city.

I stared, wanting to intervene, but I wasn't acting.

I was a frozen sabertooth in a cave while the caveman was murdering the caribou.

The woman pushed the man away and started yelling.

The man swung the boxcutter at her.

She stumbled away.

A look of realization crosses her face.

She punched the man in the mouth.

She dug her nails into his right arm.

Then… he stabbed the woman.

I was still too unable to act, my mind disagreeing with my body.

The man stabbed her three times before I yelled to scare him.

"Hey!" I yelled.

Why did I yell it…?

"Who the fuck are you?" He asked me.

"I'm gonna-- stop you," I told him, more or less stuttering.

I was trying to make him nervous, unstable. That would give me an edge over him. That would help with the size difference.

"Fuckin curry munching midget wannabe superheroes," he swung the boxcutter at me.

Midget?!

I backed up, barely dodging it.

"You really-- suck at this." I was still slightly stuttering.

The man pursed his lips and lunged at me.

I smacked his right arm where the woman had clawed at him.

He dropped the boxcutter and half-curled up in pain.

I kicked him in the leg.

He fell to the ground.

I grabbed him.

"Wait-- You're that Leto boy. Son of those billionaires-" The man said.

He smiled.

"Your momma-- how many surgeries look like that? She looks like one of the dumb whores I'd kill and rape-- Oh man what I would give to cut her wide open and--" He spoke as he attempted to get up.

I grabbed his boxcutter from the floor and
forced it through the side of his neck.

"Don't talk about my mom," I told him.

I stared at him.

"That's sweet... you're a momma's boy." He choked out calmly, trying to claw at my face.

Then he looked into my eyes, the old man and he started freaking out-- his eyes widened, he squirmed erratically, trying to speak, but only gurgling came out, and his head shook back and forth.

After a few moments, he stopped squirming.

I'd realized what I had done.

I killed him...

Crap...

But I mean he was a killer!

I looked over and noticed the woman wasn't moving either.

She was dead, judging from all the blood, she... bled out, obviously.

I heard a scream.

It was my boss.

I realized that it would look like I killed the woman too.

"Wait boss, no-- I--"

9

My boss pulled out her phone.

There was a slight noise.

My boss fell to the floor.

"Who's there?!" I yelled and held up the knife.

She walked into view with her silenced pistol.

She saw all of it.

Jamie Freeman.

11

Officially she was hired by my parents to watch over me.

But she's more of my Aunt.

More of my best friend.

She's really nice, caring, and pretty.

She has some sorta superhuman training or something because I've never seen someone her size move so fast, jump so high, and have so much stamina.

In the heat of the moment, I guess… I got distracted?

To be fair, she can also be very quiet.

"I've got you, kiddo. Don't worry, we'll handle this." Jamie told me.

"What?" I asked.

"I was watching the whole time, but I thought you would just beat the man down and become a hero like you wished to be, and if there was any chance you'd get hurt, I had my gun trained on the man and would have killed him. I hoped being a hero would cheer you up from what happened at school, so I took a chance, my job and life-- or you being sad."

I should have been more…

Scared?

Scared of myself for killing someone?

Scared that I'd get caught?

Scared that I wasn't scared?

She instructed me to follow her.

I was silent.

With Jamie's guiding eye, we used some of the store's supplies to clean the blood off the floor.

I made a few taps on my watch.

And the cameras went to static.

For the whole day.

…

The man had been buying the same stuff every day for weeks.

Several women have disappeared on this block every night that he's been coming in.

No bodies were found.

All from my city.

Where the buildings, which reach as high as the Tower of Babel would have been, and keep the streets in the dark with their shadows.

Darklind.

Where everyone is either greasy rich or bare bottom poor.

Where murders, rapists, thieves, and muggers are commonplace roaches and rats who breed like rabbits or possums and love the night like bats.

But, did that make what I did right?

If he was a monster who stalked and killed women?

But if he's a monster, what does that make me?

Why was I playing judge, jury, and executioner?

I realized I was in a car.

She was driving.

I broke my silence.

"Jamie, this isn't the way home."

The Road Home

"Jamie, where are we going?" I asked as she drove.

I just wanted this day to end.

"Leto Chemicals." She told me.

"What? Why?" I keep asking questions.

"We need to get rid of the bodies, and you have access-- like you have access to most cameras in the city because they're mostly LetoTech, which your parents own. Your parents also own LetoChemicals, just like they own the store that I killed the boss of for you. There is a compound in Leto Chemicals, compound DM 1-971, that has similar components to organic bodies that can also dissolve bodies and most other things, bones and teeth included. It also becomes non-acidic and a different compound completely when exposed to water." She explained.

"I thought we were going home," I said.

"And what were you expecting would happen to the plastic-wrapped bodies in the trunk? Blood can be found, but your blood wasn't there, showing no signs of struggles that include you. You wiped the cameras too. But the bodies are still there." She rationalized.

"Oh," I said.

"You're kinda out of it, why don't we get a bite to eat? I know how you get when your anxiety acts up." She offered.

"Y-Yeah." I complied.

"I'll go in, you did enough work for today Jamie," I said.

"Nah, you need to relax more than I do kiddo. Just make sure no one goes near the trunk, the smell of blood is kinda noticeable." She instructed.

"Yeah, it makes me woozy," I said.

"Don't puke until after we get the food." She smiled.

Wait...

She left the car on so I could feel the luxury of the air conditioning.

I somehow fell asleep before she came back.

To cops knocking on the window.

"Can I help you, officers?" I rubbed my eyes.

"Son, we've noticed a strange smell coming from your trunk. Hoping you could open it?" A cop asked.

I would be fine if I got in trouble, but Jamie would go down with me if they found the body...

"Excuse me, but are you insinuating I've done something wrong? Do you know who I am?" I had to flex my money and status... Christ...

"Who are you boy?" The other cop asked.

"I'm the older Leto Boy, Karma Leto," I said.

The cop took a look at my face.

His face went pale-er.

"Would you like me to call my dad? I'm sure he can sort this out" I asked.

His face went white... er.

"N-No sir, it's just--" He stammered.

"Just what? Just because I'm brown I'm probably involved in some kinda illegal business?" I asked.

Did I really just pull the race card...? Yes, I did.

"No-- We just--" He stammered more.

"You just what? It's a car, it should smell like iron." I asked.

"So you smell it too?" He answered my question with a question.

...Shit.

I pulled out my phone.

"No need to do that sir! Our bad, we apologize!" The cops said.

They left, quick.

Then Jamie came back.

I decided I would never kill again.

Ever.

I lie to myself a lot.

"How do you know that we have chemicals like that?" I asked.

"I talk with Francis a lot," Jamie explained.

In that moment I realized...

I realized I'd have to change my license plates.

"If you pretend to have fun, you might have some."

I was at school before the bell.

I like to be early.

And so did she.

Her curly red hair was down, and her full squishy face was cute as always, littered with freckles across her cheeks and forehead.

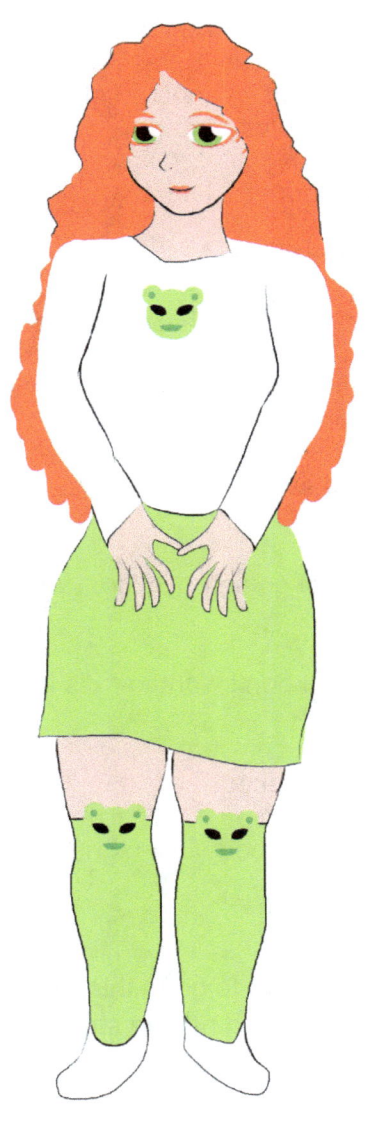

Kimber Keen

"Hey Karma! I just wanted you to know-- I thought about your confession, and I think it's worth a shot. Wanna go out this Saturday?" It was Kimber.

"I-I'll think about it," I said.

It hurt to say that.

I'd been crushing on her since 3rd grade.

Now I was in 8th grade, and I was still crushing on her.

She looked sad for a second, then regained her smile.

She had a lot going on in life, I wasn't mad at her.

"It's not that I don't want to-- it's just..." I trailed off.

"Yeah?" She asked.

"I kinda… hid a body last night."

I did not say that.

"I have a function to go to this Saturday, y'know, all that rich people stuff." I told her.

She smiled, "That's okay, and I'm sorry I said no-- I really don't know how to feel about you. Your jokes suck, but you're not

21

mean or anything. Plus the babyface is
really cute."

"Your jokes are great too, and I doubt you're
capable of being mean. I take it you're
falling for me a bit?" I asked in a joking
manner.

"Oh shut up." She laughed.

…
…

I saw Mister Loud at my house.

Mansion, whatever.

I was reading a medical textbook but put it down to talk to him.

I wanted to be a doctor.

"Hello Mister Loud, how are you?" I asked.

He stood at least two feet over me.

Tall and comforting.

"Please, call me Francis, Mister Leto." He said.

"I won't do that." I chuckled apologetically.

"As you wish sir." He responded.

Mister Loud is a soft-spoken man. His wife hits him and he never retaliates. His son hates him because he's a "pussy" for it, but Mister Loud never so much as yells at him. Mister Loud is the sweetest man I know.

My parents took him in when he was an orphan on the streets, he was trying to hotwire their car--

Correction, he did hotwire their car.

The cops caught him not too long after, but my dad was more impressed that a 9-year-old could hotwire a car.

So, they took him in, mentored him, and in time-- made him head of Leto Tech and Leto Chem.

"Uh, what's up Mister Loud?" I asked.

"Well, I am carpooling with your parents to a meeting-- but quite frankly, I have to talk to you about your trip to Leto Chem last night." He said.

Oh no…

"Oh, what about it?" I asked.

"Quite frankly It occurred to me you were attempting to not be seen-- at night it's best to wear as dark colors as you can, so I looked over our projects at Leto Tech and decided you'd want to have this for those late-night activities." He opened a suitcase.

I saw…

The darkest scuba gear I'd ever seen.

"A gimp suit?"

I didn't say that.

"Uh, what is it?" I asked, scared of the answer.

"It's a suit with a vanta black coloring, so it absorbs about 99.965% of light. This

25

particular suit is equipped with an extremely light but effective bullet-resistant plating that uses chemical bonds composed of a synthetic chemical manufactured by LetoChem. The plating is more clothlike than kevlar, and more bullet resistant, but still not bulletproof-- it is however fire retardant. This means you can move around with the suit as if it were a onesie, but with more protection than a kevlar suit and you'll be safe from fire. Sharp objects can still cut it with extreme force although the damage will generally be lessened, for example, a cut that would pierce your flesh may just slash up your skin. You will also be able to feel blunt force, although the blows will be softened to a degree. The suit also has livingel properties-- livingel is a material that LetoTech has been developing, it can be molded under certain conditions to hold its shape through a process similar to muscle memory. After being conditioned to have a certain shape, livingel will always attempt to return to its shape through the same pseudo muscle memory-- essentially repairing itself. Therefore if you get cut the suit will conceal your blood from leaving the suit. However, the suit will become thinner and less protective if it repairs itself without enough material, as it is attempting to achieve its original shape without having the necessary mass. To avoid thinning, you can put the pieces that have been removed onto the suit and let it incorporate the parts back into itself, or use a supply of the livingel variant used to make the suit. However, the suit's most useful feature for you, is that it will blend into the night, and make it difficult to see you and your features. The green lenses are night-vision goggles, to help with the late-night dives." He explained.

Did he know?

"And there are pockets." Mister Loud finished.

I should have argued that I didn't need it... because... I didn't...

"Oh-- I, don't know how to ever repay you, Mister Loud, is it really okay for me to have it?" I asked.

"Mister Leto, this whole company is your birthright. Quite frankly, you can take whatever you want. Quite frankly, I will also make any adjustments you need. If I'm not in, others should be able to assist you. Quite frankly I owe my life to your parents. Quite frankly, you are like my nephew-- Not to say, I'm above you of course! I just meant that-" He went off.

"You're fine!" I chuckled.

He always does that, he belittles himself and magnifies my family.

"And quite frankly, I'll never refuse an order from a Leto" He confirmed.

"Francis, how are ya?" My dad walked in.

"Mister Leto, I am good-- and you?" He greeted my dad.

I thought it was weird how short my dad was compared to Mister Loud, yet how strong my dad looked compared to him.

"I'm good as well, I'll be waiting in the car-- Karma, how are you kiddo?" My dad greeted me.

"I'm good dad, good luck at the meeting," I said.

He ruffled my long messy hair, "of course, your mother and I will be home late, Vale will want to take us out, as usual, you and your brother can order food, have a few friends over."

"What friends? Jupiter and Roselle moved away years ago." I joked.

And that other one, the one I try to remember sometimes, only to feel a pain in my stomach... I don't know what happened to them...

"Kimber, maybe?" He smirked.

I was silent.

I'm rarely ever silent.

My dad chuckled, "she's a good girl, you should ask her out if you like her."

"I dunno, I have that charity ball coming up and--" I tried to say.

"Take her as your date!" My dad interrupted.

"I-- What?" I asked.

"Oh sorry, your "plus one"-- but Karma, some advice, If you pretend to have fun, you might have some." My dad quoted.

"You got that from a Batman movie." I smiled.

"... The Dark Knight, right? I was more into Spiderman back in the day-- the comics, but yeah-- what's with the gimp suit?" My dad motioned to the vanta black suit.

…The what?

"Oh--" I was cut off again.

Honestly, I was going to say it was a venom symbiote costume for Halloween.

Then I realized how dumb that sounded due to the fact that Halloween was a ways away.

"Your son has taken an interest in scuba diving, I took the liberty of getting him a suit." Mister Loud said.

"Oh, thanks Frankie." My dad patted his shoulder, "now c'mon bud, we gotta get to this meeting."

Mom, Dad, and Mister Loud said goodbye
and left.

If you pretend to have fun, you might have
some, huh?

"Brobro--" I heard my brother, Harrison,

"Invite Kimber over, I'll even help you out with flirting."

"Harrison, you're not old enough to know how to help me with that," I said to him,

Granted, he looked older than me, he was the same height as me-- and stronger than me, he's abnormally muscular for a 9-year-old. Our family doesn't grow very tall, but we can gain muscle easily. We also take long periods of time to lose it. Our dad hasn't worked out in nearly a decade, but he's still relatively strong, although much less than before.

"I'm old enough for Ellie Waller," Harrison told me.

"You are not dating Ellie Waller, she's 13," I said.

"I never said I was dating her." Harrison shrugged.

Date?

I did invite Kimber over.

"So, I know you-- but I feel like I don't know you-- who are you Karma Leto?" She asked.

"Uh-- I'm a wannabe superhero." I panicked.

"Everyone knows that dork, c'mon, tell me something no one knows." She demanded.

"I'm a momma's boy." Kimber smiled in that way that said, "he's so cute, but he's so dumb."

"Why do you like me anyway?" Kimber asked.

"Hmmm, I want to be like you."

"Oh, you're trans? Or do you want to wear my skin? Both are fine. I just need to be ready--"

I smiled at that.

"Personality-wise, you know you like being alone, but you care for everyone, and you don't care if anyone accepts you. I want to be like that. I used to think I'd like to be alone. Because I thought that if people got

33

close to me, they'd just leave. So, I didn't want people to care for me, and like me. Only you. Also, you love my jokes, but I digress. Also, you're one of the only people I know that's shorter than me."

She laughed, "yeah, your jokes are pretty okay."

"Wow, you are down astronomically bad for me aren't you."

We shared a laugh at that.

I saw my brother Harrison mouth the words, "invite her."

"Uh, Kimber!" I said louder than expected.

"Yeah?" She responded.

"Would you like to be my da-- plus one?" I asked.

"Plus one?" She asked.

"There's a charity ball coming up-- Dancing for the Damaged-- I wanted to know if you wanted to go-- as friends!" I asked.

"Nah." She said,

"...Oh, okay." I said dejectedly.

"Now, if you were asking me to be your date, that's different." She smiled.

If my skin was lighter, I'd be blushing.

"Kimber Keen, will you be my date?" I asked.

"Damn right I will." She accepted.

Harrison looked happy.

I read a romance novel that night, then the medical textbook.

I was getting to the part of the cranial cavity, fun~

I had the news on, I was on the news... kinda.

"The killer being dubbed 'the Bilson Street Boogeyman' has been identified and confirmed. Several bodies were found scattered across the city, each being drunk women last seen in a bar near Bilson Street, each with the same fingerprints and DNA on them. Police assumed that the women were victims of a serial killer, but with no bodies until now, they were said to be missing people's cases. The killer has now been identified as Isaac Jackson, who has seemingly disappeared himself. His apartment was raided but there were no traces of Jackson. The camera's of the street have been mysteriously wiped, and no body has been found for the killer, and he has not been seen in several days."

I Can be a Hero

I spoke to Mister Loud again a few days later.

He was in charge of my event attendance, if I wanted to bring Kimber as my plus one--

My date…

I'd inform him and he'd inform the ball people or whatever.

"Uh, Mister Loud?" I walked into his office.

His face lit up like it always did when he saw me.

"Mister Leto! How are you sir?" He shook my hand.

"Okay, before we talk about that-- a detour, why do you care about me so much?" I asked.

"Is it not obvious?" He asked.

I said the smartest thing I could, which was "uhhh."

"I see that same drive in you to help people that I saw in your father-- that day he saved me and over the years he took to make me who I am. I tried to hotwire his car, and he saw that he could help me, hone my skills, make me better, and he did. Like him,

37

you're a good person, Karma, and good people are the best-- they're everyday heroes." Mister Loud explained.

I said, "I-- Uh-- Ok" like the word factory I was.

 I was just letting you know that I'm bringing a friend to that ball." I said.

"Oh, a date?" He asked.

"I mean..." I trailed off.

"Karma, we don't know what happens after death-- if there's nothing, we only have one shot to do what we need and want to, are they your date?" He asked.

I paused.

"Yes." I said.

He smiled, "that's my future Boss."

"So uh, you think I can be a... hero?" I asked.

"Quite frankly, Mister Leto-- the only thing that can limit what a Leto can do is his own will to act. And often that fails too. You're very, very smart Karma, you skipped a grade despite the fact that you never and still don't study for tests, you just casually do your homework. You could even own the world in a few years if you want to." Mister Loud hyped me up.

What I Do Defines Me

I had Jamie's bodyguarding given to
Harrison.

She didn't seem happy about it, but seemed
to catch onto why.

She also started training me when Harrison
was sleeping and I wouldn't.

Combat, getting out of situations-- hero
stuff.

She was trained to be able to survive on low
amounts of sleep like me, just not as much.

I memorized the routines to train when
Jamie was bodyguarding Harrison during
the day.

I hadn't killed since that night.

I did, however, visit where the bodies lost
their lives.

I knew it happened, but I did it anyway.

Even with that man dead, the killings went
on.

If I hadn't...? Then maybe the mountains of
bodies under my feet wouldn't be there
today.

If I hadn't, they'd all be alive.

But if I hadn't, there would be more oceans of innocent blood.

I killed a killer, but there were others out there.

The police were kinda useless at this point.

I can't save everyone, but I sure as hell had to try.

Anyway, a few nights later, I was walking around Darklind.

I saw a boy from my school in an alley, it was a shortcut.

Max.

"You're bad baby." A man said to him.

"Leave me alone." Max said.

The man grabbed Max.

"I like when they're bad." The man said.

I grabbed a wine bottle from a trash bin.

"Then you'll be head over heels for me." I said.

I hit him in the face with the wine bottle.

The bottom of the bottle shattered off.

"I'm gonna kill you, you psychotic pretty motherfucker, and that boygirl, right after I rape-" I snapped and slashed his throat open with the remnants of the bottle.

That's two.

"Shut up. You won't touch him." I said.

"You good?" I asked Max, trying to act like I wasn't... I don't even know what emotion it was.

"Did you just kill him?" Max asked.

"Y-Yeah. Are you good?" I stuttered.

"Yeah..." Max said.

"Good, you're not gonna tell, are you?" I asked.

I wouldn't have hurt him if he said yes, he's innocent.

"No I won't-- thank you," Max said.

He was strangely calm about it all...

I smiled, "you're welcome."

I walked Max home.

"So, who are you?" He asked on the way.

"I'm that pretty mofo. You?" I asked.

He laughed.

"I'm a freak," Max told me.

"Not really?" I raised my brows.

"Dude, you know I'm a girl, right? I just want to be a guy." Max raised a brow.

"You're a boy. It's biology versus psychology. Sex is your chromosomes, that's biology and it can't currently be changed-- but gender is your mental identity, and usually-- but not always-- how you present yourself, if you identify as a boy you're a boy, and if you identify as a girl you're a girl. Besides, even biologically,

43

female and male brains are structurally different, and generally, transgendered people have brains more similar to that of their perceived gender. People who say otherwise generally don't know the scientific differences between sex and gender. Trans folk are just people who were born into the wrong body-- and I mean intersex people exist too-- plus you're cute regardless of your gender." I said.

"You're cute too-- but I like girls," Max said.

"That's chill. Me too." I said.

"So what about if someone identifies as an attack helicopter?"

"You can identify as one, not sure how you'll present yourself as one. I mean you could just pour gasoline into your ass and jump off a building." I said.

Max laughed.

"...You killed someone for me. Why?" Max asked me after he stopped laughing.

I thought about it.

"...People are defined by what they do. I wanted to be defined as a hero." I said.

"Heroes don't kill."

"Eh, I'm atypical."

44

I opened my watch and wiped data in the area for the last few hours.

I dumped the bottle-- the murder weapon, in chemicals that broke it down into untraceable goo.

I'd come back for the body later with my suit on, wrap him in plastic wrap, put him in my car, dump the body with acid.

I'd be doing that a lot.

Even if I left the body, there was nothing to tie me to his murder, I never touched him, I didn't touch anything but the bottle.

The blood however would make it obvious that the missing man was attacked, but there would still be nothing to tie me to it.

But still, the cameras were wiped.

The bottle was gone.

My prints weren't on anything but the bottle.

And there was no body.

Unless Max spoke, no one would know who killed the man, or if the man was necessarily dead.

And if he did speak? I don't think I'd hold it against him anyway...

I mean, I slashed a man's neck with a broken bottle-- although I feel most people would think of doing something similar to a rapist.

Everyone was thinking it, I just actually did it.

If you don't think of it, I applaud you.

If you do, I ask, is what I'm doing really that bad?

Actually-- don't answer that if you're genuinely enjoying this story.

We all have some inner darkness, mine just makes up all the dark matter in the multiverse.

But it's okay friend, you're safe in these pages.

Just don't kill anyone, I'm not a role model-- at all.

The Night of the Dance

If a group of hedgehogs moves close to each other to share heat during cold weather. They can't, they'll hurt each other with their sharp spines. They all want to be close, but they can't.

Arthur Schopenhauer came up with that.

Kimber is the first human being I've ever really even been close to in years, apart from family.

I am a literal murderer.

What if I hurt her?

No, I'd never hurt her.

Would I?

"Hey Mister Keen-- I'm here to pick up Kimber?" I greeted the tall man with sandy black facial hair but brown scalp hair.

"Hey Karma, come on inside."

I admired the Keen's Christmas tree, it wasn't super tall, but it was cute, and modest.

You could argue it was up too early, it was only November.

I put something under the tree.

Then I saw her in the dress, her long hair was tied into a bun, her lips were outlined in red, her long eyelashes even longer due to makeup.

I mumbled, "She's worth the risk"

...

I thought it would be classical music... It was dance music.

They even played music by Corpse.

That night--

I had no idea how to dance.

Years ago my Mom had tried to teach me, but I didn't want to.

Mom didn't push it.

"C'mon Karma, dance with me," Kimber said, somehow vocally clearing a jump over the music.

"I don't know how to," I said.

"Just move around! C'mon, I'm practically begging!"

I got out of my seat.

That night, I looked like an idiot, and Kimber didn't seem to hate it.

That night, Kimber laughed, and I laughed.

That night, I had fun.

But I knew it wouldn't last.

Because serial killers don't get happily ever after.

But I'm not a normal serial killer.

I'm better.

Bully

Mister Loud's son, Conner, was bullying a kid at my school.

It's an all-ed school, so all grades congregate in one building. Conner was in like 11th grade or something.

I put my hand on his shoulder, I just wanted to talk to him.

He punched me in the face.

He started hitting me over and over.

"What, you think because your daddy is my dad's employer I won't break you?" He asked me.

I was getting ready to hit 'em in the face with that special move--

Harrison pulled him off me and pushed him against the lockers.

"Actually yes. Leto Enterprise ain't as clean as you think. We can make you disappear-- and no one will be able to do anything about it-- we have the money, the power, and the influence. Don't touch my brobro again. You don't want to go missing right before school lets out and miss your summer vacation-- because you're tied up and gagged in a room thirty feet underground with soundproof walls." Harrison commanded.

Conner had no words.

Harrison let him go, and he ran off.

Kimber appeared and helped me up, "you good?"

"Harrison, what did you mean when you said we're not clean?" I asked.

"I was bluffing dumbass." Harrison walked away.

Kimber rattled my arm.

"I'm good Kimmy," I said.

"Don't call me that!" She acted angrily.

I let out a chuckle.

...

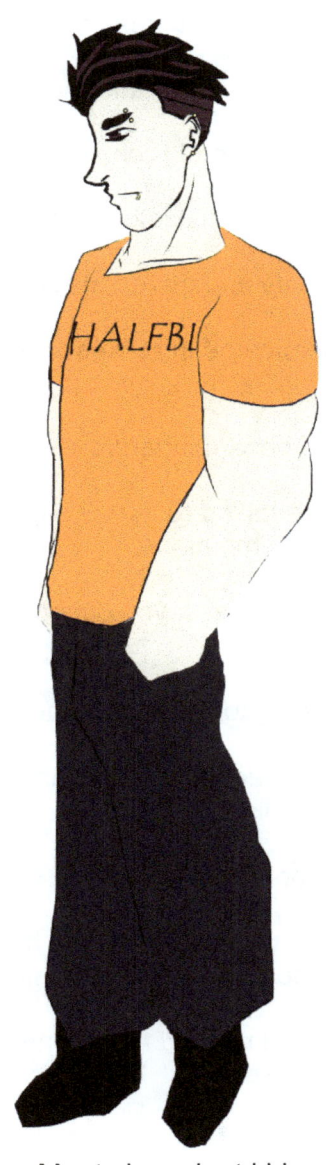

Monty is a giant kid.

And Rick is a gigantic freaking kid.

Rick attacked Monty's girlfriend, Shelly.

Then, Monty slapped Rick.

Rick smashed his fist into Monty's face.

I caught Monty and glared at Rick.

The teachers came in and escorted Rick out.

Monty and I became friends.

More like, he talked to me all day and wouldn't leave me alone.

"That was so badass, you caught me like a superhero!"

That was going to go to my head.

"Just don't expect me to fly in and save you all the time, Lois."

We both shared a laugh at that.

At the end of the day, he asked for my phone number, and I gave it to him.

The next day, I noticed that Monty's bag was extra packed.

"Karma-bro, watch my bag?" Monty requested.

I agreed, and Monty went to the bathroom.

I knew how unstable Monty was from yesterday, I had to check.

Door locks.

Monty came out of the bathroom, I had zipped back up his bag.

"Monty, don't lie to me-- what are the locks for?" I had seen a movie.

"I'm not gonna shoot up the school like Kevin did in that movie if that's what you're thinking. I swear it-- you know I wouldn't lie to you Karma-bro."

"What are they for?" I asked again.

"Just know that I won't be shooting up the school, or doing anything wrong, I promise. I'm too scared to kill myself, and jail ain't much better." He told me.

Monty has said in the past that he's tried to kill himself but just couldn't go through with it… To teachers… Who did nothing about it…

I'm paying for this boy's therapy. I don't care.

School Shooting?

On the last day of school for 8th grade, I was walking to the cafeteria. I didn't eat as much lately, but I had promised Harrison that I'd try to eat more.

Then I saw the crowd.

Around the lunchroom.

"Oh no..." I muttered and pushed my way past the crowd.

Monty wasn't lying, he wasn't gonna shoot up the school.

But Monty had locked himself in there with Rick.

Rick was tied to a chair.

"I'm gonna kill you Monty," Rick said.

"Yo-- shut up." Monty smacked Rick across the face.

"Monty stop!" I yelled.

Monty looked at me, then grabbed Rick's head and slammed it on the floor.

"What's your deal psycho? What do you want?" Rick asked, his mouth and nose bloody.

"I want you-- dead." Monty grimaced.

"Go for it, baby." Rick smiled.

Monty grabbed Rick's face and put it on the chair.

I held my watch up to the lock.

It was LetoTech.

It opened.

Rick looked at me for a second, "my knight in shining armor," he smiled.

"Shut up Rick," I said.

"How did you-- open the door?"

"Mister Zachariah helped me," I said.

"He's been missing for 3 years?" Rick asked and said at the same time.

"Yeah, don't end up like him," I said.

Then I grabbed Monty's hand and ran.

We ran out of the school.

I'd minimize the damage. But Monty would likely need therapy or go to juvie.

"You're a real idiot-- you know that?" I scolded Monty, "what was your endgame? You were gonna kill Rick? What then? Life in prison? What about your future?"

Monty said something I didn't expect.

He laughed--

"What future?" He asked.

"What are you talking about?" I was lost.

"Karma-bro, my old man split years ago, and my mom is dead. I'm in foster care. I'm 17, no one adopts a teenager. I have no job. I have crippling anxiety all of the time-- which can only be quelled through doing dumb crap to feel alive, like trying to murder Rick or protecting people, I'm sick of the latter, and the former is illegal. Karma-bro, I'm detrimental to society, whether I die in jail or live on the streets, either way, my life ends in June." Monty said.

"Listen, if you kill someone-- I will have to take you down," I told him.

"And I won't hate you for it. We're the same." Monty said.

"I wish we were." I wish I was clean of the blood on my hands.

I have a future.

Would I really ruin it by killing again?

Is it already ruined?

I patted him on the back.

I knew that act left him with something that would bring us closer. Maybe it'd help me stop him if I needed to.

Maybe it was just metaphysical, but it'd be enough.

4 Weeks of Hell

Ever hear of Junko Furuta?

The 44 Days of Hell?

It's probably the worst series of atrocities ever committed on a single human being.

Unfortunately, I don't live in Japan, so I can't go and cut up the perpetrators right now.

I mean I have several planes, and it's summer vacation…

But basically, this guy asked a girl out, and she said no. He was such a little bitch that he and three other equally worthless high schoolers, captured the high school girl, and kept her captive for 44 days.

They raped her repeatedly, till she was pregnant. They tortured her in disgusting ways, like putting a lit light bulb in her vagina, and even fireworks. They burned her down there with lighters too. Then they killed her after getting butthurt over losing some game against her because they're bitch ass babies.

Then they put her body in cement and nearly got away with it. Somehow.

Rest in peace to Junko Furuta, you did not deserve any of that.

I can't help but be unnerved at the fact that cruelty like this rarely happens to men in comparison to the amount that they happen to women.

Then again, males have this standard where they don't speak of sexual abuse or mental health issues, but sexual abuse does happen to males, and we can be mentally ill.

But I've never heard of all of the hell that happened to Furuta happening to a single male, much less one in high school, the rape, the torture, the mutilation, the captivity, etc.

Not all in one case I mean.

The reason for this whole rundown is that I stumbled on a copycat of the boys from the 44 Days that summer.

Monty and I were eating lunch in the courtyard of the school.

I overheard some kids talking-- I'd seen them around the school before, "Yeah, Rick's keeping her at his house. She's basically a slave."

I had a reason to murder Rick now.

He deserves it, right?

Rick was already a clear delinquent, but I had no specific reason to murder him until now.

Maybe I'd just beat him to shit and call the police?

A hero would beat them up and call the police.

But I've already killed two people...

I showed up at Rick's house at midnight, wearing my vantablack suit.

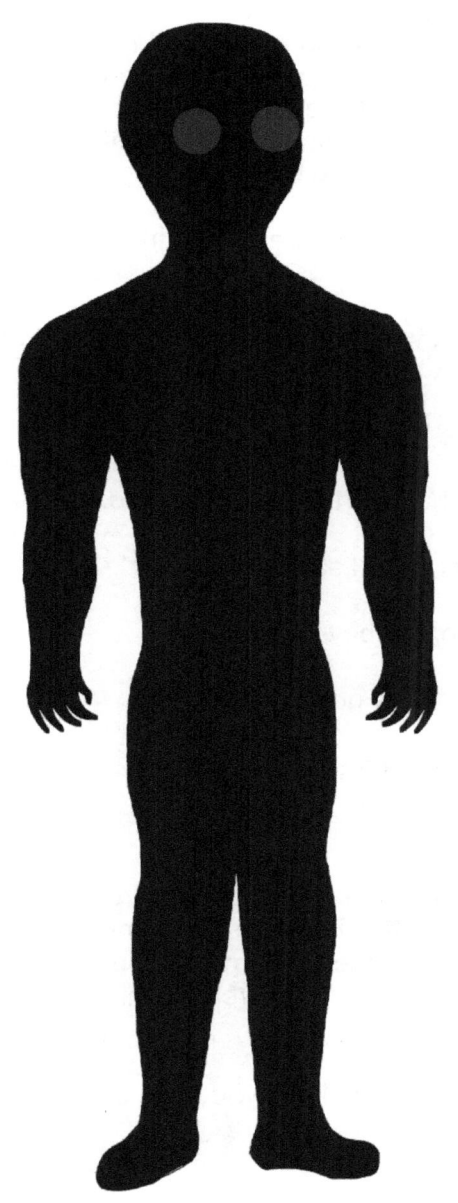

It masked me from head to toe, my long black hair tucked into the helmet which covers even my mouth, my brown skin was unseeable. My eyes were behind a mesh, I have super dark brown eyes anyway, to the point they seem black.

A group of boys were smoking at the entrance, do these kids not sleep?

"Dude, what the hell are you supposed to be?" A boy asked.

"Move," I said.

"Or what shortstack?" He asked.

"I'll kill you," I said.

One of the boys got up.

He pulled a gun.

I had to be fast.

So I was.

While moving my head away from the gun, I put my left hand on his wrist, my right on the barrel, I pushed inwards, snapping the gun out of his hand and breaking his pointer finger.

"Where the fuck did you learn that?!" He yelled.

"It's called quick thinking. I assume you're incapable?" I said.

Jamie actually taught me, but that sounded cooler.

"What do you want?" He asked.

"I want... to save the girl," I said.

"So what-- you think you're Batman?" He asked.

I pointed the gun at him.

He backed up real fast.

"Batman doesn't kill, I kill. Now move out of the way before I cap your face." I demanded.

The other boys looked shaken too.

He waddled out of the way.

"Where's the girl?" I asked.

"Inside, we'll take you to her-- just chill with the gun." He told me.

"Walk." I demanded.

He led me inside.

"So are you really a kid?" A boy asked.

"Walk." I repeated.

I expected them to attack me.

I wasn't ready for what I found.

Holy shit.

"What the hell did you do to her?" I took the mask off, not sure if it was due to pure shock or if I wanted to be sure I was seeing correctly.

Rick had captured Laney Doman, he and his crew had been torturing her for the entire summer, I knew that.

But, Laney's stomach was bloated, she was beaten, bloodied, and blue. Her wrists were bound so tightly that her wrists were purple. She was in a cage.

The other boys were already gone.

I heard a click…

"Don't fire that," I said.

"Shut up, raise your arms, and turn around." It was Rick.

"Aight." I did.

He shot me.

I flew back.

Then I got up.

67

The suit is bullet resistant, it probably wouldn't take too many more rounds-- if even one.

"Oh god--" Rick was shocked.

I took advantage of his confusion.

I dug my fingers into his side and he toppled over.

So I smashed my fist into his nose.

His face changed from sure of himself, to terrified.

"You're... one of them? Why are you doing this? What are you gonna do to me?!" He asked.

"I'mma save the girl. I'm--" I froze, then regained my composure "-going to flay you open and dissolve your body in a vat of chemicals-- after I get her to the hospital." I was in control.

So much so, that I tied Rick up with a rope I found in his basement and left him there.

Suicidal

"Why didn't you let me die?" She asked me as I drove her to the hospital in my car.

Yes, it's my car, I'm a filthy rich teenager who can bend the law-- I have literally killed people, how is this a conversation?

"I only let people like Rick die," I said.

"They're already gonna come out damaged, I can't abort them, I'm Catholic... my shit family will never accept them either, more like they'll bully them until they..." She explained, then broke into tears.

"Have them then, your lord will figure out a way." I said.

"Who are you?" She asked through sobs.

She didn't see my face, it seemed.

It was dark in there...

We didn't speak for the rest of the ride.

I think her faith was broken anyway.

I think I was actually going to tear a few of Rick's body parts off before flaying him open.

...

When I returned to the house I found Rick with his wrists slit open.

He was dead.

Thing is…

There was no knife.

Also, I didn't do it!

I assumed the absolute worst and hoped I was wrong.

Monty.

Based on GPS tracking of Monty's phone at the time, he was right outside the house when I went in...

And went inside when I drove her to the hospital.

I rewinded the GPS records and Monty had been following me that day.

But, was what Monty did really wrong?

I was gonna kill Rick anyway.

Rick was a disgusting vile piece of shit.

Maybe I'll give Monty a pass here.

No…

This could only end one way.

With one of us dead.

Me or Monty.

You can't know someone is a killer and just leave them to roam free.

Unless like, you're contractually obligated to them, like Jamie-- or Mister Loud, I think?

Or if you have whatever the hell was going on with Max.

Granted, he was an accomplice for not turning me in.

But I didn't want to kill Monty...

I'm a monster, but I'm a caring monster.

And he was my friend...

Bigger Bad

"Did you kill Rick?" I asked Monty while holding a knife.

"I did bro." He admitted.

"I had to dump the body and burn the house down. Furthermore, I warned you-- I have to make it right." I said.

"You think you're a killer too?" Monty asked me.

"I am. I've killed two people already." I revealed.

"Then we're in this together." He told me.

"What?" I asked him.

"I'm a superhero, and you're a superhero too." He rationalized.

"We're killers Monty, we're not superheroes-- if anything we're villains!" I yelled back.

There was silence.

"Say you'll stop Monty," I demanded.

"And if I don't?" He challenged me.

"I'll kill you," I told him.

"I like it, I like avenging people, I like saving people, and I like when I'm in control, why do you get to kill but I don't!?" He yelled.

"Because I can handle it, you're a good guy Monty, you'll break." I explained.

"My brother, Karma Leto, is the sweetest kid in school, what makes you think he can handle being a serial killer superhero!?" He asked.

"I'm not a superhero, I'm a killer because I'm good at it. I can kill. I kill killers." I said.

"Me too." Monty suddenly walked towards me and spread his arms, a knife in each.

I panicked.

I already had a knife in my hand.

I dashed and slashed his neck open.

He looked surprised for a second.

Then he smiled.

"At least I'm not gonna kill anyone again… Looks like... I was... the villain, huh brother?" Monty choked out the words.

I hardened my face, "We're just killers, and I'm just the bigger bad… brother." I told him.

…

I wonder if there was a bigger bad than me, an enemy I'd have to overcome to take my place at the top.

…

Well, that makes three.

In the span of three months.

If I was caught now, I'd be considered a serial killer…

I assume I'll just be changing my license plate a lot from now on.

But for now, I won.

I always win.

But there was no one to accept me, again.

And he was right, why do I get to kill but not him?

I noticed that the knives he was holding were on the floor where he had held them only moments earlier.

He had dropped them while walking towards me.

I was scared, and I didn't notice…

I fucked up.

…

Two people from my school were missing.

I knew Rick's gang wouldn't talk.

The main suspect in the case of the disappearances was Monty, they thought he had killed Rick and fled the area. Makes sense seeing the events in the lunchroom.

There was also Karl Tylers.

He's a victim turned monster, still a monster. Rick used to bully him until Karl got the size to match Rick. They fought a lot after that.

Pretty sure Karl roofies girls too… I'm curious as to whether Rick had any part in him doing that.

Note to self, slit Karl Tylers jugular… and hit him with something heavy… in that order.

There was also Luka Tonfa, a teenage delusional narcissist, who believes that no one can stop him, so he should just do what he wants. He used to kill animals when we were kids. He just wants to win at everything at all costs.

Rick broke Luka's dad's leg at a father-son race just to win. Which I found strange because Rick didn't have a dad.

Of course, the true perpetrator was Monty.

But, no one needed to know.

Deaths Before the Darkness

School started back.

It was fall.

I was a 9th grader, 13 years old.

Pictures of me in my vantablack suit
surfaced.

Then again, the twenty or so pictures
people have of me couldn't be traced to me
unless they found the suit.

The cameras were wiped, but people take
pictures when they see people dressed in a
costume that looks like it was made of a
black hole.

I was a fugitive living a life of luxury.

I paid for Laney and her child to start over
far away.

I'd wire them a couple thousand every
week.

It was all I could really do for them.

I wasn't going to make her go against her
religion, even if I didn't agree with it.

Of course, I made the payments
anonymous.

Harrison was doing a football team thing.

Jamie showed up at the mansion.

"Hey, Jamie--" She tackled me.

I struggled, but by the time I made the slightest iota of sense of what was happening she had me in a chokehold.

I was gonna fight back but...

I couldn't.

This was my best friend.

Then I passed out.

...

I woke up in the safe room in dad's main building.

Jamie sat in the corner.

"Your parents are dead Karma, you're next." She told me.

"Why?" I asked and grabbed an m9 from the rack and pointed it at her.

I was shaking.

She looked hurt.

"I didn't kill them, and I have to make sure no one gets to kill you." She stared at me.

"What's going on Jamie?" I asked.

"I don't know, but I think the safest place for you is in this building." She explained.

I was silent as she strapped up, guns, knives, gear, and armor.

Then she walked to the door.

"Where are you going!?" I asked.

"I'm going to protect you." She said,

"No!" I yelled.

"No?" She asked.

"Stay here, with me-- what if they hurt you? What if they kill you?" I asked.

She was quiet for a moment.

"Then I die protecting my best friend." She hugged me.

"Please don't go, Jamie." I pleaded.

At this moment, I wasn't Karma Leto, the serial killer.

I was Karma Leto, the scared 9th grader whose best friend in the world was his bodyguard.

"It'll be okay Karma, I'll handle this." She said,

She walked out the door, locking it behind her.

And I heard gunfire.

I ran to the door, unlocked it, and saw three dead men.

And Jamie, bleeding out on the floor.

"Jamie!" I ran to her.

"What the fuck is wrong with you?!" I yelled at her, "You work for me-- doesn't mean you die for me!"

"I took a chance, my life-- or yours. I've always told you, I've got you, honey." She choked out.

People were running down the halls.

I let out a scream.

It wasn't a badass growl or a psychotic yell, it was a scream, a child's pained reaction over losing someone he loved.

I was crying, but the tears didn't fall, even as the world crashed around me.

I tried to force the tears, to no avail.

This was my best friend, and I couldn't even cry as she died.

It wasn't toxic masculinity, I haven't been able to cry for years.

But I really thought this would be my breaking point...

It wasn't.

Some part of me is just dead.

Something is missing.

It might sound cool to never cry.

It's torture.

I don't know how it died, or what killed it.

I know that it makes me a massive piece of worm shit.

Anyone who says "men don't cry" is lying, and shouldn't even call themselves a man.

They're closer to being a bitch.

And I'm not using the term bitch in equation with being a woman.

When I say bitch I mean insecure pathetic people.

See, not crying because you're a "man" is just being scared to express your emotions because you're scared people will see you as weak.

A strong person doesn't care how others see them.

They know they're the shit.

Me? I don't care how people see me.

But I also can't cry.

So I'm not sure what I am.

A man or a bitch?

I don't think I'm a woman, so it's between those two.

Then again I'm 12.

But spoilers, the tears will come, give it another book, maybe a few.

Because things don't get better.

They get so much worse.

Alone in the Darkness

Mister Loud closed Jamie's eyes, his men secured a perimeter around me.

He held me as I stared at her corpse.

He assured me he'd guide me through everything.

But I couldn't be guided if I couldn't see anything but red.

As I stared at Jamie's corpse, I thought about what happens when I'm scared.

If I wasn't scared, I wouldn't have murdered Monty.

Maybe I could have fought on Jamie's side, and she'd still be alive.

I decided something.

From now on, I don't get scared.

From now on, I make people scared.

…

I don't like funerals. So I don't go to them.

I was to inherit Leto Enterprise when I turned 18.

Katie Myers was in control of my company now.

She was my guardian now, along with Harrison's.

We decided not to burden our Grandparents.

But, even with all that money.

All that power.

I was alone in the darkness.

With mere candles to light my way.

Four had already gone out.

Mom and Dad.

Jamie.

I visualized Monty.

And I realized, I shouldn't have killed him.

And I added that to my list of mistakes.

But I had a few lights left.

I had Mister Loud.

Harrison.

And Kimber.

And my lighter still worked.

But, I still couldn't see anything at all.

I wasn't in control of my life, and it irritated me.

I was no detective, and it'd look suspicious to start right after my parent's murder, then if the people who killed them were dead right after I started looking...?

I have to be smart about this.

Then I'll kill them discreetly.

My big bad enemy boss.

She Doesn't Love Me

She saw right through me.

I wanted to be rid of her as soon as
possible.

I had to kill my parents' killers, I couldn't do
that with this freakshow following me
around.

She knew me when I curbed the kid that
was bullying my brother.

If my family wasn't financially top-class, I'd
probably have gotten in trouble.

But my parents paid the kids' parents off,
and I was let off.

This girl, however, witnessed what I did.
And I'm sure she remembers it, even after
moving away and back.

Hannah Ramcharam

She kept following me around, talking to me.

"You have a boyfriend," I told her.

And she was taller than me.

"You have a shadow." She said,

"Doesn't everyone?" I asked.

"I mean an inner darkness, that's eclipsed by your light, making a shadow." She explained.

I thought her wording was strange, but I didn't critique it.

"I'm no homewrecker," I told her.

"I think you misunderstand-- I find you interesting, I want to be your friend and analyze you. You wanna go to a Lakeview party?" She asked.

"Why would I want to hang out with those kids?" I asked.

"I wanna see if you'll snap again." She explained.

Can she see through me?

We went to the stupid party.

For the record, I hold my alcohol like a champ.

9 beers back-to-back without getting tipsy in the slightest.

I can do more though.

Then I saw a guy feeling up Hannah.

"Hey-- chill, she has a boyfriend," I said.

"Nah Karma, it's all good." Hannah basically moaned, clearly drunk.

There's too many people to kill the guy.

No wait, that shouldn't be my first instinct, I only kill horrible people.

But isn't feeling up a drunk girl with a boyfriend, being horrible?

Then I heard him.

"Kill him," Monty said.

I almost smiled, then I felt a wave of fear and my blood dropped to absolute zero...

"It's not really me dumbass, your brain is buggin out-- I'm a projection of your subconscious," Monty told me.

"Oh ok, it's just you," I said to the psychological eldritch abomination in my head, my PEA if you will.

Wait no-- don't call it that.

Jesus Christ, I am literally losing it.

Where did it go?

Did I ever have it?

But I knew I couldn't kill this guy right now.

"I gotta go," I said.

"But Karma, babyface, the party's just starting!" Hannah basically moaned as she said it.

I dipped.

Pimpin Ain't Easy

I needed to… hurt someone.

I was so… upset!

It was this itch in the back of my head.

My leg was jumping.

"Dude, he was basically date raping her. Kill that fucker, and laugh at his funeral." Monty said.

I already killed three people, do I really want to kill anyone else?

"I want to, but what? Am I supposed to drag him out of the house and kill him?"

"Hey man, I'm just a projection of your overactive mind."

A newspaper got stuck in a fence near me.

I saw the headline.

Neo Jack The Ripper.

...Jack the Ripoff.

Prostitutes were being murdered.

You can say what you want about the profession, but there are many reasons women sell their bodies. It doesn't make them evil.

Sometimes it's to support themselves or loved ones.

Some women are sold into it.

Some women are basically brainwashed.

At the end of the day, prostitutes are people.

They don't deserve to die because they have sex for monetary gain.

There needed to be some sort of justice here.

A mediator.

Karma.

So, I started hanging around a pimp to find the Ripoff.

I was underage, but I was absolutely rich, so he turned an eye.

Then Kimber saw me with some girls.

"What the fuck Karma!? Am I not enough for you?" Kimber was pissed.

"That's not it!" I insisted.

"Then why? Why were you hanging out with them? Is it because they're just great people?" She questioned me.

"I--" I froze up.

"You?" She asked.

"I just have to do this-- I can't tell you why..." I said.

"Of course, the billionaire boy has reasons that no one understands-- like wanting to get laid and having the money to pay women for it!" She yelled.

"That's not it!" I yelled back.

"Whatever, come back to me when you get a sense of morality." She walked away.

I noticed something as she walked away.

My serial killer lifestyle did end up hurting her.

My quills stabbed her.

I really can't get close to people without hurting them...

Mentality

I noticed the killer's type.

Black hair, blue eyes, pale skin, early 20s.

That's my type too, one of my many types…
Or maybe I don't have any types? Maybe I
just like everyone?

Anyway, the truth behind it all was so
bizarre, strange, and nonsensical.

I may have been blatantly tagging several
prostitutes through questionable methods,
cry about it.

Tracking chips are illegal to use on humans,
right?

But jokes aside, The Ripoff was a prostitute,
who killed other prostitutes.

Okay, that's hilarious coming from a killer
who kills killers, but still.

Speaking of secrets that no one would ever
be able to fathom as possible in reality,
Kimber isn't talking to me.

Kimber was taking a psychology class with
Hannah.

She and Hannah were friends now.

I don't know what Hannah told her, but
Kimber came up to me one day.

"Hey, I'm sorry for saying what I did-- I know
you have a side of you that needs to do
certain things, things that I can't fulfill
completely-- I'm just scared you'll get
yourself hurt. But I'm not mad at you
anymore. Just be safe. Wear safety."
Kimber said.

"Oh, ok," I said.

Wear safety?

Oh dear god…

"What did you tell her?" I asked Hannah.

"That you're a sexual deviant, is there
something else that I should have?" Hannah
asked.

"A sexual deviant?!" I asked.

"Karma, just accept who you are," Hannah
told me.

"I am not a sexual deviant," I said.

"Then what was that at the Lakeview party?
I've been keeping tabs on you, childhood
trauma can lead to sexual deviance; it's not
your fault-- and Kimber understands that!"
Hannah explained.

I was lost.

I guess she was that drunk.

Cause I didn't have sex with anyone at that party.

And I wasn't sexually abused, I just stomped a kid.

Holy shit, she confused me with the guy at the party.

She had sex with him.

"You should cut his dick off, kill him, and throw him down a flight of stairs... in that order," Monty said.

"Obviously dumbass, I was gonna kill him anyway-- he was a predator regardless."

"I know," Monty said.

"Yeah-- uh, thanks, Hannah." I didn't press it.

"I got your back bro." She said to me,

I smiled.

I don't know if it was a real smile, or a fake smile, and if it was the latter, was it out of fear? Or just to blend in? Who was I lying to? The world or myself...?

All of the above, definitely all of the above.

Roselle

I was at a bodega.

I try to live normally, okay?

So, a while ago, I stopped remembering my past when I realized moving forward is all that matters.

Then I saw her, and things came flooding back.

White hair, messily tucked into a black beanie, presumably dyed, but I've never seen her roots in a different color and she's poor so I don't think she can afford that much hair dye.

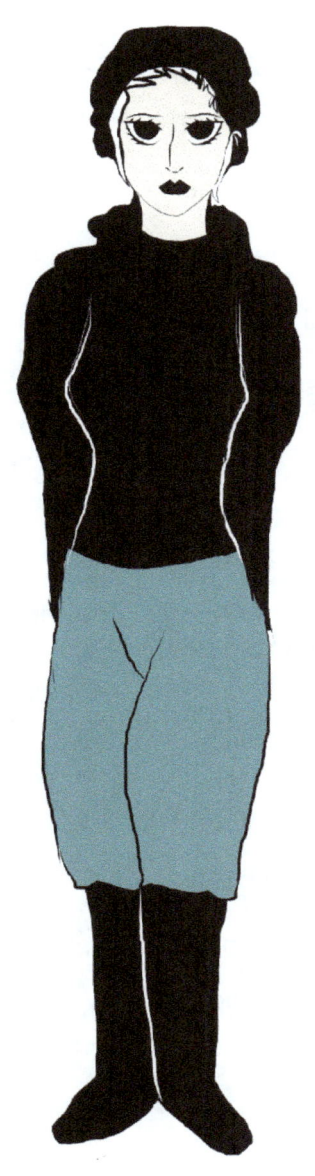

Rosellus Bells

98

Roselle.

Ross.

"Ross?" I greeted her.

She was still taller than me.

She looked panicked for a second.

Then she smiled.

"Karma, how you been?" She recognized me.

"I-- What are you doing here?" I asked.

"Dad and Mom divorced, I'm living here again." She explained.

"Where are you gonna go to school?" I asked.

She would go to my school.

I was happy about that.

"You're going into 10th?" I asked.

She's a bit older than me.

"Yeah, you too?" She asked.

"Yep." I said.

"Lit. I gotta help my father move some stuff--but I'll see you tomorrow. Kay?" She stated and asked at the same time.

"Ye." I smiled.

Powertrip

Over the course of a few days, Roselle and I rekindled our friendship.

I never asked about the others, I didn't really care.

Roselle looked prettier than usual one day.

Roselle and I were getting food.

Then it started raining.

Now, I would gladly walk in the rain, but I didn't want Ross to get sick too.

Roselle pulled out an umbrella and handed it to me.

"Hey, look at that, enough room for us both." She said,

"Ye." I agreed.

Only about five minutes into walking home the damn wind blew away our freaking umbrella.

I looked at the sky and shouted, "eat shit!"

When I looked down, Roselle was dancing in the rain.

She actually looked happy.

She didn't care about anything, she was just happy.

Then I noticed something...

...

Bruises across her forehead.

A huge one around her right eye.

She looked at me, "ever notice that if you wear clothes and get soaked it's like your clothes are hugging you?"

"What happened to your forehead-" I grabbed her by her wrists, and brought her close to me for inspection.

More bruises, across her arms.

Even a few on her legs.

"What, happened?" I wasn't angry, I was just really concerned.

I was kinda angry.

"Dad. It's been going on for years. In every way. Kinda surprised the genius didn't figure it out."

Even Monty was quiet.

Her eyes...

Her eyes were emotionless and unsettling.

"And why haven't you called the cops? Or killed him!?" I asked.

"Because I'm 16 and I would have nowhere to go. I don't wanna be some orphan in a home. If you can't keep up with what life throws at you, you should just die." She said,

This gave me deja vu…

"Then I'll kill him," I said.

She looked unimpressed like she thought I was talking hot with no explosion to follow.

"No, I'd be put in foster care. And no one adopts a 16-year-old." She explained.

"Then what? I just let your dad keep abusing you?" I asked.

"Yeah." She said,

Once again, I felt powerless…

The Ripoff

Valencia Gorgon.

The Ripoff.

I didn't care for the why anymore, I just wanted to kill someone on my terms.

As she started her car, I wrapped a wire around her neck.

We were in a dark area, so she couldn't see my face through her rear view.

"You're gonna answer my questions." I was slightly curious.

"Why do you kill? Aren't you and the local prostitutes like a sisterhood or something?" I didn't know jack shit about prostitutes.

"I kill.... to feel loved by more men." She explained.

Now that's an unusual motive.

"If I'm the only one to sleep with-- they all have to pick me." She explained.

I let go of her.

She didn't turn the lights on.

We sat in silence.

I wanted to help others, without anyone feeling love for me.

She wanted everyone to love her, while helping them.

Were we more different or similar?

She still didn't turn the lights on.

I walked out of the car.

But before I walked away, I said, "no more."

The Karma Killer

I think knowing that I made her stop was
enough control.

I felt better.

Someone gave me the name The Karma
Killer, without knowing it was me.

And it stuck.

Some people put it together that the guy in
the chaos black suit seen in the area that
people disappeared from was probably on
some illegal shit

Some people pieced together the fact that
only bad people went missing. Hence the
"Karma" part.

I also left bloodstains, the "Killer" part.
Granted, it can't be proven that I killed them
due to no bodies being found, the fact that
my DNA isn't traceable due to me wearing a
full bodysuit, and the fact that there is no
footage, but people assume things.

I kinda killed Rick's gang too… That's why
they wouldn't talk.

My parents greatly helped the more
marginalized people of Darklind.

After their deaths, most people were pissed,
scared, on edge, etc.

The city itself became very unstable, like it was off its meds again.

People had started assaulting and sometimes even killing criminals on their own.

I guess they saw my actions as a call to fight.

"Hey Karma Killer!" Someone yelled.

Shit.

"Nah, imagine, the rich boy being like a serial killer Batman? With the dead parents and money I mean." Hannah's giant boyfriend, Jake Deblas said.

I resisted busting his head open.

"Holy shit Jake, you can't say that shit," Hannah told him.

When did she get here?

"Oh, sorry." Jake apologized.

That's right, Jake isn't all there in the head.

"You're good bro," I told him.

It's in my name you bumbling idiots.

...

The police were getting nowhere with the investigation.

I really miss them, all of the dead who I held close to my heart.

Too bad it doesn't beat anymore.

But how can I be a serial killer Batman if I'm no detective?

Well, I actually got my first lead by accident.

The Foodie

I saw Felix Thomas crying in the hallway at school.

I saw Kimber approach him.

"Lix, what's wrong?" Kimber asked her.

"Archie is gone!" He said.

"What do you mean gone?" I asked.

"They took him!" Felix said.

"Who took him?" Kimber asked.

"I don't know, my dad owed a debt and I think he pawned him off. He didn't come home last night!" Felix explained.

I knit my brows.

Lix's dad is a scumbag who constantly dips in and out of his kids' lives.

Maybe I should kill him? He deserves it…

First I gotta get Archie back though.

I left school early, and broke into Felix's house.

I turned on his computer.

Mister Thomas probably used it when he was around.

I logged into Mister Thomas' email.

I didn't even have to hack it, it was saved.

He owed a good 8k to a man who went by the username "FoodieFanaticPhantasm."

The latest email was yesterday.

"Meet me at the slaughterhouse, I have your payment." Mister Thomas had sent.

I went on my phone and searched "FoodieFanaticPhantasm."

Shu Melo.

Suspected of murder, but never charged.

They found no bodies.

No murder weapon.

But Mister Thomas owed 8k to him, Archie disappeared, this guy was suspected of murder, and the email was sent the night Archie disappeared.

I think I'd heard of the place before too.

I decided to go to the local slaughterhouse at 3 AM.

And, Shu Melo was there, I recognized him from pictures in the articles about the murders.

He seemed familiar somehow.

"Shu!" I yelled.

"Mister Leto?" I heard a voice, "did you get surgery? You look younger."

Was he making a joke? Or did he not know of my parents' death?

"I'm his son." I said.

I was confused.

"Oh, well, come in." He said.

"I'm in, where's Archie?" I asked.

"He'll be right out. Your dad didn't eat my stuff, but I'm glad you came by." He said.

I narrowed my eyes.

"What? I'm not hungry, I want to know where Archie is." I said.

"Oh I see-- hold on, I'll bring him out." Shu agreed.

I was ready to kill Shu, but first I had to know.

He brought out a burger.

Getting closer to being sure.

"A burger?" I asked.

"It's Archie," He said.

"He's in the burger?" I asked.

"Yeah, some of my best work, the kid's flesh was so soft and tender." He boasted.

"You killed Archie and made him into food?" I asked.

"I thought you knew--" He started to speak.

"Hey watch this--" I said.

I shot him in the leg.

Monty was smiling in the booth across from mine, "feed this fucker to the pigs!"

"Motherfucker!" Shu yelled.

I grabbed him by his collar and dragged him to the back of the slaughterhouse.

I tried putting pressure on the wound first.

I wanted him to suffer.

The blood felt weird--

So I cauterized his wound…

With a blowtorch.

He passed out, so I jabbed him with a syringe I took from LetoChem.

"You have some serious fucking problems!" He yelled at me.

I don't like being yelled at.

"I'm not the one eating people! You have a problem!" I yelled back.

"I have no problems, I have a fix-all solution." He insisted.

"And what's that?" I asked.

"Eating." He said.

"Fucking what?" I asked.

"Anything can be solved with eating. Sad? Eat. Angry? Eat. People don't want to be your friend? Eat them. Wife carved up by some mugger? Eat them. Girlfriend killed by the mob? Eat them." He explained.

"And why eat Archie?!" I yelled.

"His dad owed me-- I collected, I'm a cannibal, it's what I am. What are you, some kinda superhero? Avenging some junkies kid?" He asked.

I looked at my hands.

Stained with blood.

"I'm something like you-- Hungry, with an endless voracity, for something that can't be justified. I'm something wrong and horrible, flawed and sick, evil and dark. Something that has to feed to survive."

"Then I'm sure you're capable and want to feast on your parents' murderer?" He asked again.

"Yeah." I said again.

"Listen, his name is Valendro Mozkiv, your daddy's company has an underworld faction to it. I serve Valendro when he comes here, he owns the place it's been in his family's name for years-- I heard him-- he personally gave the order. They're business partners, your parents tried to shut down the criminal factions, the board tipped off Val, and he did what he had to. I've made sandwiches for Mozkiv. You don't want to cross him. Pull down my pants." He said.

"The fuck you got going on?" I asked.

"Just pull it down, I want to show you the leg that's not the one you emptied a bullet into." He instructed.

"If it'll shut your cookey ass up--"

I did.

It was a prosthetic.

"What happened?" I asked.

"Valendro cut it off and made me cook it-- just because he wanted to know what a human who eats humans tastes like-- he's no ritual cannibal, but he's a monster among monsters and has no restraint. He loves learning, he's smart, he will hunt you down, and slice you apart, just like he did mommy and daddy." He was pushing my buttons.

"Why did you make me pull down your pants?! You could have just had me pull it up!" I yelled.

"I wanted to fuck with you."

"Better question-- you stayed working for him?" I asked.

"I had no choice, I could go to Pluto on the only ship that could transport a human there and he'd get me," Shu explained.

"He will die, even if I die killing him," I said.

"You don't listen to people, do you? You are your dumbass parents' kid." He was pushing the giant red button that says "do not press this giant red button."

"Stop talking about my parents," I said.

"Or what? You'll kill me? Both my legs are fucked-- you'd be doing me a mercy." He smiled.

"No-- you don't deserve a death from a human, you'll die to your own kind," I told him.

"And what's that?" He asked.

"Pigs," I said.

His face went white.

Monty did a dance.

I shot Shu's leg again.

Opened the pigpen.

And watched as they ate him.

I heard him screaming, I felt...

... Nothing, at all.

I just stared.

What is wrong with me?

Oh well.

I wiped the cameras.

Scrubbed the floor.

And took the prosthetic leg and threw it in
the acid.

I'd come back for whatever remained of him
in the excrements of the pigs, and possibly
the bullet.

The Gougeman

I started visiting the gangs of Darklind, I had been cutting down on my killer calories for a few weeks at this point.

But as I had taken a break from murder, others made it up for my deficit.

Naturally, as people started assaulting and killing criminals, the criminals fought back.

So the assailants started vigilante gangs, they needed to fight in numbers to survive.

And the criminals did so as well, in bulk.

Criminal gangs and vigilante gangs started fighting.

I mean, vigilantes are criminals...

Anyway, I had single-handedly started a multi-faction war-- by accident.

There was the Karma Cult. The collective of gangs that came about as part of The Karma Killer's actions. They violently executed those they deemed guilty.

The Demons Saints of Darklind. A step down from the brutal murderers, this teenager gang just assaulted criminals, violently.

The Street Slasher Saviors. They did what the Karma Cult did, but they didn't cite the Karma Killer as their inspiration.

And so many more.

No one was ever sure as to which murders were The Karma Killers, as no one had ever caught me-- or had too much evidence. And now with the mass of all of the same-motivation murders, it just became harder to discern who did what. Even when police did convict one person, there were ten more unsolved cases.

The only evidence The Karma Killer even existed were when I was wearing the suit near where people were last seen, and people took pictures.

But I was taking a break, which meant no more pictures were surfacing.

Somehow no one had ever gotten images of me with a body.

Maybe some people even thought I was caught, or killed.

Then there was my copycat.

The Gougeman.

They gouged out the criminals' eyes.

Over twenty ex-convicts-- dead.

Thing is, the eye-gouging didn't kill them.

Blood loss did.

The killer gouged their eyes out without killing them immediately, and let them die from bleeding.

The Gougeman seemed almost superhuman in his precision.

I decided I'd team up with The Gougeman to kill Valendro Mozkiv.

I also had to crush Leto Enterprises' criminal branch.

I'd do it legally, once I took over the company.

I spent a while searching for The Gougeman.

The Gougeman is the Karma Cult's unofficial leader, he didn't start the gangs or take over, he doesn't give commands, but they say they owe it all to him. That if he gave the word, they'd destroy Darklind itself

But no one ever sees him. They just call him "the killer who went on," after The Karma Killer took a break.

He could just have been me operating under a different identity.

I couldn't even find him.

120

He was so ridiculously careful, so precise, and clean. He was the perfect killer. Apparently, no one ever saw him and lived, no one that came forward at least.

After some time I gave up on finding him.

I figured if The Karma Killer started all of this, his return could raise his status back up in the eyes of the vigilante gangs.

Who doesn't love a reboot of a good story?

And with the gangs, I'd have the army required to take down the Mozkiv family.

But they wouldn't believe it was me just because I wore a suit.

I had to kill.

The Tooth Thief

A cop showed up at my house

I left my watch upstairs.

"Someone with control over Leto Enterprise technology has been wiping data from cameras in view of several crimes." The cop said.

"Really now? Any leads?" I feigned innocence.

"No, we were hoping you could help with that." He said.

"Well, Leto Enterprise tech works less like a network, and more like a plug and play. If you have a certain technology you can control any Leto Enterprise technology, but we don't link our products to a central server, it makes it harder to hack us. What's more is that we don't use logs on these devices, and they use a local communication connection as opposed to wi-fi or 4-and-5G. Like a walkie-talkie." I explained.

He thanked me and said he'd be in touch.

His name was Officer Rumi.

I saw another killer on the news.

The Tooth Thief.

He's less of a murderer and more just a sicko.

He drugs people, takes their teeth, and runs.

Apparently, he was less important than most criminals, so the cops left him alone… or just suck at their jobs.

Good enough, I'll kill him.

…

Okay, this asshole was so sloppy I'm embarrassed for the police.

I knocked him out, tied him up, and took him to a warehouse.

"How haven't they come for you yet? You're sloppy and not even white." I said.

"What?" He asked.

"Sorry, policism," I said.

"What?" He asked.

"I discriminate against cops," I explained.

"What do you want?" He asked.

"To kill you," I said.

"You like hurting people? Then we're alike!"
He said.

I paused.

"...Yeah, I honestly love it, but I also like
helping people. I gotta be kinda selfish
right? I'm not perfect, I'm a person. A
terrible person, who kills terrible people." I
said.

"You help people to feel good about
yourself. You're still selfish, like me! You're
a psychopath!" He proposed an idea.

"No, I help people because I like seeing
people happy and because I like killing
abusive assholes-- like you," I said.

"So you do it to satisfy yourself! You take for
your own sick gain!" He yelled

"Maybe you're right, I take from the guilty by
hurting them. I give to the innocent by
hurting the guilty. I gain from the innocent
without hurting them... although I suppose
your family might miss you... might... Oh
well." I dropped a crate into his head.

I made a peace sign into the camera with
my suit on, then wiped the data, except for a
frame of me making the peace sign with the
dead body in the background.

A Roadblock?

The governor was proposing replacing Leto Tech cameras

Of course, this would cost the city a lot, money, partnership with Leto Tech, and the support of the people.

People didn't exactly hate that The Karma Killer was killing criminals.

So it never passed.

The gangs flocked to calling The Karma Killer their co-leader.

And the mayor went missing anyway.

Good enough.

Teen Drinking is Very Very Bad

Kimber was at my house.

We were drinking.

We broke into my parents' alcohol room.

She knocked out on my couch.

I decided to take a nap on my other couch.

I woke up to see someone wearing my suit!

I freaked out.

"Karma--" It was Kimber, she hiccuped.

"Look, I'm the Karma Killer-- But I'm not like other killers--" She said and passed out again.

I had to get the suit off of her, if she comes to, and isn't too piss drunk to forget that I have it-- I might be fucked.

I took the suit off of her.

Then she woke up as I was putting my mom's clothes on her.

She slapped me.

"Jesus Christ Karma! I know you're hypersexual, but date rape?! Really?!" She screeched.

Hypersexual? I'm a whole-ass virgin!

"I am not-- I was just trying to get my suit off of you!" I realized I said that after I said it.

I was kinda tipsy...

I drank a lot.

Shit.

She looked at the suit on the floor.

"Are you--" She started to ask.

Fuck.

"Are you the Karma Killer?" She asked it.

I couldn't lie to her.

I also don't really try to hide it.

"...Yeah." I explained with one word.

Take me to Church

She…

Invited me to church.

She was hoping I could find and stop a killer.

I went a few times.

After the first time, I started doing some Biblical reading and research on the general times when the books were written.

Problem is that the original manuscripts the Bible has been derived from have been altered and rewritten too many times to count and most versions are pretty biased and have been altered to fit different narratives.

Unfortunately, I don't know Hebrew, Aramaic, or Greek to the point I can read the Dead Sea Scrolls or the original New Testament manuscripts…. Shit, I should really get on learning those.

So for the Old Testament, I read a few different translations, including the King James version for a traditional version, and Young's Literal Translation for… literality.

As for the New Testament, I had to read several translations, as they're more up to interpretation and I am not fluent in Greek and Hebrew to the point I can properly read anything reminiscent of the original documents.

Among the others I used for the New Testament was the New Revised Standard Version.

I was very rusty on theology, so I had to do some advanced speed reading and consume a lot of caffeine.

Waging war on a mafia could wait.

I wanted to make Kimber happy.

And maybe I could save myself.

Get better?

Wait, but then who would destroy that mafia?

Maybe the gangs would do it by themselves?

Killing this one could also just help strengthen the idea that The Karma Killer is back.

That Sunday, someone asked one day, "Pastor, can murderers reach heaven?"

"Everyone sins, but those that repent of their sins, and give their lives to the Lord may enter the gates of heaven. Even murderers."

"So, can someone just keep killing people and ask for forgiveness every time?" I asked.

An old man chimed in, "It works more like that if you're truly sorry for what you've done, you can be forgiven."

The Bible does not say that.

There isn't a verse that says that you have to be sorry, just that you have to confess and repent.

So, Hitler could enter heaven if in his last days he did and meant all of those things?

I don't like that thought.

A sensible god wouldn't allow Hitler into heaven, but I don't think the Bible says that Yahweh is a sensible god.

Then again, didn't Jeff Dhamer do that shit? Supposedly?

"And, can Jesus heal someone who is broken inside? Like, completely shattered and battered?" I asked.

An usher chimed in "My parents said I had an inner darkness. I was a troubled kid. Drugs, sex, all of it. But now thanks to the church I'm a new man!"

Yeah, but I assume you weren't cutting people's throats.

Apparently, despite the fact that people from the church were being murdered, people didn't stop coming.

It was kinda admirable, if not just blind and foolish.

Granted they were being killed in their homes.

I wasn't sure if it was faith, but they hadn't been doing anything harmful that I've noted.

My philosophy is to let people have their religious beliefs as long as they're not being harmful with it.

"Why do children in foreign countries starve to death if Yahweh is real?" I asked.

"That's what has happened to their civilizations as a result of their own actions. You can't blame God for the actions of man, we have free will."

But I'm supposed to credit him for every good thing that happens?

And the Pharaoh had free will, but then Yahweh hardened his heart-- because somehow that makes sense-- couldn't he soften Elon's heart? For the children?

"Okay, but if god supposedly cares about people so much in first-world countries, hearing their prayers and whatnot, why not those third-world children who are dying? I heard people claim that God cured them or helped them through hard times, but it's always in a properly developed country-- never in a place filled with poverty, even when people pray and hold onto hope as they should." I said.

"The Bible says in Exodus 20:5 that 'the iniquities of the fathers are visited upon the sons and daughters — unto the third and fourth generation." The Pastor.

It also says "The soul that sinneth, it shall die. The son shall not bear the iniquity of the father, neither shall the father bear the iniquity of the son: the righteousness of the righteous shall be upon him, and the wickedness of the wicked shall be upon him." in Ezekiel 18:20, so that's a direct contradiction.

It sounds immoral to torture babies because of what their parents and ancestors did.

If you have the power to stop a murder, and you don't, you're an accomplice.

So if you have the power to stop torture, and you don't you're helping to torture.

If you can stop suffering, and you don't, you're helping to cause suffering.

And every country is full of sin, especially us in America-- founded on genocide and conquest, built on slavery-- oppressing through segregation-- and we still have massive bouts of depravity and racism.

I let it go.

Most Christians are too indoctrinated to let go of their way of thinking, some will even die over it.

And I can't even blame them, they were taught these things from birth and during formative years, it's ingrained in them psychologically, they're conditioned from childhood and it's not even their fault.

Breaking it generally calls for trauma, some level of intelligence, and interaction with unindoctrinated people who can think for themselves.

"So what exactly would it take for God to be considered evil?"

"He can't be evil."

"I dunno, I find killing Job's family as part of a bet with Satan is pointless and evil."

Especially considering there was no need for the bet. According to what people believe, God is all-knowing, so God knew the outcome and how Job would react-- and why would he have a bet with Satan? The supposed personification of evil? His worst enemy? That's like when Mister Krabs had a bet with Plankton, and he bet Spongebob's entire existence.

I also find it laughable when people say things like "God can't be held to human standards" despite the fact that being like God is meant to be the basis of human morality.

I also find it hypocritical that in the supposed "Biblical" story of Lucifer-- which never occurred in any Bible verses if you can properly read-- Luci was cast out of Heaven because he wanted to be like the being God, but humans are supposed to aim to be like God. Lucifer wasn't aiming to be God, he just wanted to take his title of God. It's like becoming President, Joe Biden didn't actually become Donald Trump. He just beat him in the elections and took his place.

Speaking of Lucifer being cast from Heaven, according to Job 1:6, Satan can totally still enter Heaven, "Now there was a day when the sons of God came to present themselves before the Lord, and Satan came also among them."

Snap back to reality--

"He created us, he can do as he sees fit." The Pastor replied.

Close enough.

"So if I created a new lifeform, I have all the right to murder, torture, and do other disgusting things to them as much as I want, because I created them?"

"God is pure love, he'd never do those things."

He tortured Job by killing his family and taking everything from him-- he gave him a new family in the end but that doesn't.mean that Job's first family came back to life-- they are still dead-- this shows that Yahweh sees human lives as objects that can be taken and replaced.

And the millions of people he killed in the Old Testament alone can argue with "God being love."

See, often in the Bible. When Yahweh goes on his killing sprees for any reason a kill count is given.

And it adds up to over 2 million.

Events such as the supposed flood along with Sodom and Gomorrah aren't included in that 2 million, as they had no given death toll.

But the flood alone is thought to have been about 20 million.

Pure love, huh? According to how some Christians act and claim-- that's as long as you're not gay or trans.

Like Westboro Baptist Church-- the degenerate hate group.

I let it go through.

But I had another question.

"So, what's the plan for the starving children in all these suffering countries? To die? That seems like an evil plan." I told him.

"God works in mysterious ways, you should ask him when you go to Heaven." He used another copout.

Also, I don't think I'm going there.

But if he allows babies to starve to death while supposedly healing other people who don't have it that bad in comparison or have had full lives in comparison to literal infants? Y'know, in these so-called miracles that people say still happen? I don't think I want to go to heaven.

I mean, all they do up there-- In the words of Anthony Devon Griffin AKA LongBeachGriffy-- is pray, and watch Good Times.

The Bible also says we'll be praising God in heaven, why would I praise a god that kills babies, but doesn't kill the rapists, racists, and murderers? Why do I have to do his job for him!?

I'm also sure there were babies in Sodom and Gomorrah, and Egypt.

Why doesn't Yahweh kill any murderers or rapists with sulfur and fire like he's said to have done with the entire cities of Sodom and Gomorrah?

It's also interesting that he apparently stopped doing these things the second cameras were invented.

Also, I exist.

And if I go to Heaven how would I be happy knowing that there are people I love in Hell?

If you can only feel good emotions, that's kinda like brainwashing. Are you even human at that point?

I refuse to renounce my humanity.

And I'd rather burn in hell and get the chance to beat up Hitler every day for eternity down there than worship a god like that.

Then again, what sense would it make to send people like Joseph Stalin, and people who just don't follow Jesus because he has given them no reason to, to the same place?

Or maybe Yahweh just abandoned humanity because-- again in the words of Anthony-- people think that he white.

I wouldn't blame him, if my creation whitewashed me, I'd probably just flood the Earth again.

Wait he promised against that...

Okay, so when is the sun supposed to enter its red giant phase, and then swallow the Earth in flames?

7 billion years?

I'd speed it up if they whitewashed me.

Anyway, the murder weapon is always a bird talon.

Notes are left, they claim they are a Holy Dove, that he kills to let people fly to their destiny in the sky.

So it was someone who was allowed into the homes of people of the church.

So it was the Pastor.

I put on my suit which I was keeping in my car.

But as I followed the Pastor to his home, he got a call.

He started crying.

I took off my mask, slipped on my normal clothes over it, and pretended to be on a jog, just happening to run into him.

"What's wrong Pastor Maxwell?" I asked.

"Oh, Karma. Another has been murdered. I'm trying to keep my church calm by lying, saying that these people were sinners, to give them a sense of security that they'll be okay. But it breaks me inside. And how can I make it to heaven with a liar and a slanderer's tongue? When will this end? Will they all die? I'm supposed to lead them to be Christlike-- instead, I'm just being a demon myself..." I said.

"Are you sorry?" I asked.

"What?" He asked.

"Do you regret lying to them?" I asked.

"I do." He said.

"And your God is a just god right?" I asked.

"Yes." He agreed.

"Then I'm sure he can bend the rules when needed. He's pure love and ever-loving, right? I mean, some people kill themselves due to things that push them over the edge, things they can't control-- Robin Williams killed himself due to a mental illness. It made him unstable and he couldn't help it--

I doubt that man went to hell if it exists. He was pure. God is just. God loves his children or something. And you say that we can only blame man for the actions of man, but then shouldn't we also praise man for the actions of man, like comforting your church folk who have entrusted you with their faith that they'll be ok?" I didn't believe what I was preaching to the preacher, but this man was so broken up. He deserved to be reassured.

As long as people aren't hurting anyone in any way, what's the harm in letting them do and believe whatever they want?

Now, when you're causing death in destruction, like using the name of your god to justify slavery, invasion of a whole continent and the genocide of the people, racism, homophobia, transphobia, and stuff like that...?

That's a problem buddy.

...

I actually didn't do anything, I saw the usher entering someone's house.

I thought that was weird.

Then I saw him attack her with a talon.

I rushed into the house.

He had stabbed her.

I got him in a chokehold.

I choked him until he passed out.

I ran over to the woman.

She was dead.

I tied him up.

"Who are you?" He asked when he woke up.

I put my mask on, and my normal clothes were off.

"The guy who knows you're the Talon killer, the guy who's about to kill you," I said.

Monty was sitting in a corner, watching.

"Talon killer? I'm a Holy Dove, I kill to let people fly to their destiny, to help others!" He yelled.

"No, you're a basket case using your religion as a guise to be a monster. It's basically what they did with the Muslim religion to make Al-Qaeda agents feel justified in terrorism. They twisted around scripture arguably more peaceful than the Bible until they found a way to pervert it into an excuse to be evil. Like Christian abortion clinic bombers. Or that whole Salem Witch Trial thing. Or the crusades. Or slavery. Or Donald Trump in a more political and less directly murderous sense. Or the Spanish Inquisition. Or the founding and colonization of America." I explained.

"Then what gives you the right to kill me?" He asked.

"You killed people. You're a sinner. God killed a bunch of sinners." I said.

"You're not a god." He said.

"True… Allegedly." I reasoned.

"You're the Devil." He said.

I considered it.

"The devil only killed 10 people directly in the Bible-- 7 as part of a bet with God where God gave him permission, because somehow that makes sense. God directly killed at least two million people. I can be the Devil, yeah sure. But Satan just means adversary, so I'm the adversary of evil." I explained.

"You're insane!" He said.

"Nah bro, I'm ahead of the curve, I have my own circle. There's a triangle behind me too…" I agreed.

"Jesus Christ--" He said.

"Lord's name in vain, that's a sin."

"Just kill me!"

"Kay," I stabbed him in the face.

Seven times.

I put the bodies in my car.

Burned the house down.

And wiped the cameras.

I can't be saved, I'm too far past that line.

I am addicted to murder, and being "saved" won't stop me from doing what I want to do.

Assuming that God exists at least.

…

The Bible teaches annihilationism. The Bible never says that you burn forever, it says the flames burn forever. Even early Christians believed that, that's why being rejected from Heaven scared them so much.

The text says you die a second time. Only the Devil, the Beast, and the False Prophet burn forever.

"And the beast was taken, and with him the false prophet that wrought miracles before him, with which he deceived them that had received the mark of the beast, and them that worshipped his image. These both were cast alive into a lake of fire burning with brimstone." -Revelation 19:19-20

"And the devil that deceived them was cast into the lake of fire and brimstone, where the beast and the false prophet are, and shall be tormented day and night for ever and ever." -Revelation 20:10

The Devil's angels may also burn forever, that's never clarified. They do however go to Hell.

"Then shall he say also unto them on the left hand, Depart from me, ye cursed, into everlasting fire, prepared for the devil and his angels:" - Matthew 25:41

"He that believeth on the Son hath everlasting life: and he that believeth not the Son shall not see life; but the wrath of God abideth on him."- John 3:36

If you're burning in Hell, you still have everlasting life, you're just in pain forever.

"And do not fear those who kill the body but cannot kill the soul. Rather fear him who can destroy both soul and body in hell." - Matthew 10:28

If your soul and body are destroyed, you cease to exist.

"And these will go away into eternal punishment, but the righteous into eternal life." - Matthew 25:46

Being wiped from existence is eternal punishment. You stop existing forever.

Regardless, according to the inaccurate modern Christian narrative, it's said the Devil punishes the souls of the damned in Hell.

Well, so do I.

I'm just better at it.

And I'd love nothing more than to cease to be, then I wouldn't see them whenever I closed my eyes.

What She Warranted

I called Kimber over.

She vomited on seeing Talon's body.

"Kimber--" I stepped to her.

She shrunk back in fear.

"I thought you wanted me to kill him," I said.

"I wanted him dead, not mutilated beyond recognition!" She argued.

"But I--" I tried to speak.

"You are insane!" She yelled.

"... Do you accept me?" I asked.

"What?" She asked in response.

"If insane, would you accept who I am? Can you still love me?" I needed her to say it, just her.

"Karma, you're a murderer-- a serial killer-- you kill people--." She said,

"Kimber, please don't hate me. I love you."

"I-- gotta go, I'll see you at school." She ran off.

She didn't accept me.

146

No one did.

I figured that being a killer is what drove people away.

At the very least, it drove away the one person I wanted to be with forever.

It also just ends up with people dead.

So I decided my next kill would be my last.

And if I failed on the big one, then I'd be dead, and that wouldn't be so bad.

Murder the Mozkiv

I put on my suit and mask.

My army and I tore through the nightclub.

As my people were shot down, more raged forward.

There were hundreds of us and only a few dozen of them.

I got to the boss' room.

He was eating some kinda meat.

This was my big bad?

"Hey Val." I said.

"And who are you?" He asked.

"I'm the son of billionaires that you had killed," I said.

"That doesn't narrow it down much." He said.

I wanted to shock him.

So I pulled off my mask.

"Oh hey kid. I can guess why you're here..." He said.

He fired a bullet at me, it hit me in my right eye.

"Fuck!" I yelled.

He folded his arms behind his back, each hand holding a gun, and slowly walked out of the room, into the riot in the club.

He was cocky, he was leading me outside when he had two guns and could have had a shootout with me right there.

I got up, put on the mask, and followed, the scent of my blood filling my helmet, along with my actual blood filling my helmet.

I shot at him.

He ducked behind a bar.

He fired a shot back at me, this time it just threw me back.

I got back up to see him calmly walking out of the club.

I followed him.

I shot him three times in the back.

He dropped.

This was my big bad?

Pathetic.

I walked over to the body.

And fired five more shots into the body.

Monty was standing next to me.

And then, the police arrived.

I didn't run.

I decided dying in jail wouldn't be that bad,
hell, maybe I'd just get the electric chair.

Return to Darkness

But, then I got a text.

They were going to blow up Leto Enterprise headquarters.

My parents' legacy.

I did run.

I assume the police didn't see me at first, and eventually, I was too far away for flashlights to see me.

Eventually, I saw Leto Enterprise HQ.

And was tased as I approached the building.

When I woke up I was chained up.

So that's what that feels like…

There was an attractive, tall lady, and two men armed with several guns.

I noticed they removed my suit, I was in my underwear.

The lady drove a knife into my right hand.

I sucked my teeth in pain, "shit!"

Then the lady sat on my lap, and put another knife to my neck,

She leaned in and whispered into my ear "you killed our leader, now we're gonna kill you. Anything to say?"

I smiled, "Honestly, he was pathetic. He acted like a badass until the end, but all I needed to do was empty a few bullets into his back, and he dropped like any regular man."

She pressed a knife into my neck, without cutting it.

The knife was humming.

Shaking.

Vibrating.

"You're gonna regret that. We're gonna hurt you so bad you'll cry before we kill you." She said,

"... Uh-oh~," I said gleefully, with a smile and wide eyes.

I guess it was my obituary.

She smiled, "cheeky Lil shit."

"So, will all my torturers be attractive and sit on my lap?" I grinned.

I was halfway flirting, halfway trying to buy time to escape my chains.

But with those guns, no suit, and the window between being able to escape my chains and attack anyone, that may be somewhat difficult.

The door busted open.

I saw...

Mister Loud.

And...

No, just Mister Loud.

The woman ran at him with the knife.

Mister Loud...

Caught the knife and drove it into her neck.

The two men pulled out guns.

Mister Loud ran in front of them and snapped their necks, one with each hand.

"Mister Loud?" I asked.

"Why can't you do that?" Monty asked.

"Not now Monty," I told him.

Mister Loud tore the ropes apart.

And collapsed.

I drove us to the hospital.

He was awake, but mostly unresponsive.

An hour or two later, he mustered the strength to speak.

"Mister... Leto?" He asked.

"Mister Loud, how did you do that?" I asked.

"Drug overdosing on an experimental project." He explained.

"What? Why?" I asked.

"You are almost as precious to me as you were to your own mother and father. I swore to them that I would protect you, and I did, until the very end." He said.

"What do you mean, end?" I knew, but I asked anyway.

"Drug overdosing usually comes with repercussions, the drug I took boosts your body to unthinkable levels, but we never designed a way to come down after you take it." He said.

"But..." I started talking, but trailed off.

"Can you call me Francis? One time? I know I'm a Loud and you're a Leto and I don't give you orders but--" Francis said.

"Francis, you're not a Loud, you're a Leto," I told him.

Harrison showed up, he flew back from his
football game

Monty was quiet.

The three of us stayed with Mister Leto the
whole time.

Francis Leto… was pronounced dead two
hours later

…

I looked at the floor.

My suit...

I wasn't wearing it...

I was just going to leave it there, but then I
realized that it was a gift from Francis.

You Either Die a Vigilante or Live Long Enough to See That You're The Villain.

I went back to the hellscape Francis broke me out of.

My suit wasn't there.

I decided I'd look for it in the morning.

Needed this bullet out of my goddamn head anyway.

On the drive home, I heard on the radio that The Gougeman had been killing again during the last few nights.

But I was tired.

I'd deal with it tomorrow.

Harrison removed the bullet from my eye.

Apparently, it didn't go deep enough to do any irreversible damage, considering we have the LetoHealth and LetoMed departments.

I went to sleep.

...

When I woke up I realized I probably was the Gougeman.

I had left a book on my nightstand on the anatomy of a human head, there was a notable crease on a page that included how deep eyeballs go in the human brain.

I hadn't read the book since before I nearly lost my eye.

How long have I been fucked up?

I decided to tell Harrison.

He can keep a secret, and loves me unconditionally.

"Harry, I'm..." I trailed off.

"A serial killer? Me too brobro." He casually said then went back to his book.

"..."

"..."

"What?" I asked.

"We're all horrible in this family. We just try to do the right things sometimes. It's just who we are. Do you know how our ancestors started the business? They were criminals, then one day, they had a change of heart. They wanted to help people. So they formed Leto Corp. and turned the whole city of Darklind around. Few people know that but it's true." Harrison said.

"After seeing you curb that boy, I developed an obsession with hurting those I deem evil, then it got worse and I started killing people. I tend to try to be like my big brother after all" Harrison explained.

"Huh." I said.

"I killed the Mozkiv family," I said.

"Cool, I'm late for a date, picked up your gimp suit and put it in your dresser," Harrison said.

"Oh ok," I said.

There was someone who accepted me again.

Someone who understood me.

I wasn't alone.

Also, he got my suit back.

… Did he call it a gimp suit?

A date!?

The Call that Ruined… My Whole Day… Again

Harrison called me.

Naturally, I picked up.

"Val Mozkiv wasn't killed by backshots, maybe they felt good--" Harrison started a joke.

"Harrison," I said sternly.

"Right, well he was shot" Harrison informed me

"I fired, twice."

"Yeah, but six more were fired-- into his head-- while the ambulance carried him off-- by a sniper" Harrison broke the news.

"I didn't kill Mozkiv?" I asked, disappointed.

"Doesn't seem like it-- report says he was still alive in the ambulance. The sniper shots, which were concentrated on the ambulance-- which was moving-- are reportedly what killed him… and everyone in the ambulance" Harrison told me.

"Any idea who fired the shots?" I asked, pissed off.

"Nope, bullets weren't registered, no recent sniper purchases in the area, cameras were

159

turned off-- not by the LetoTech backdoor either-- they were brute-forced. A couple saw some guy go up the staircase, he was dressed in all black--typical-- and he wasn't super tall, about your height, more muscle--" Harrison went off on an information dump.

Oh, the couple is dead now." Harrison added that detail.

"Eh, so is Val." I decided as long as I got my licks in, I was fine with it.

What I wasn't fine with was the couple being dead.

But I was tired.

I had no motivation to be the Karma Killer.

I didn't have the motivation for a lot of things.

I preferred sleeping, and dreaming.

Psychoanalysis

I hadn't killed in weeks.

But Kimber was still staying away from me.

I mean, taking a break from murder doesn't absolve you of murder.

I never bothered to talk to her.

If she reported me and my serial killer ways, I'd be okay with it.

But she never seemed to snitch on me, as I wasn't arrested, so I just kinda left it at that-- I wouldn't want to anger her and make her want to rat me out.

I figured she was scared of me, serial killers don't live happily ever after with the person they love.

I found a friend in Hannah.

"When you see bad things you react with violence to achieve justice." She stated the obvious.

"You do what you see as necessary, but your conviction is dangerous because you rarely stop to consider if you're right or wrong." She went on.

"You just act… that's what I get from when you curbed the kid."

"Yeah but I really didn't ask--"

"And every time you've killed someone since 8th grade."

…

"How do you know?" I asked.

"The title Karma Killer literally has your name in it. You're not mentally stable. Your parents are dead. Coupling those things with the fact that The Karma Killer is obviously from our school? And that you've been doing something other than gaming with the geeks all night? It doesn't take a genius to figure it out, I'm sure others watch you constantly in suspicion. Honestly, I wasn't completely sure until you just asked the question that answered the one I didn't ask." She explained.

It's not like I try to hide it.

"Jesus Christ Hannah..." I mumbled.

"I don't think he can help you now." She said,

"Old news," I told her.

"Honestly I've been trying to figure out your psychology-- at first I thought psychopathy, but you seem to have an unusually high

sense of empathy-- also you're a child--
baby faced too. I also was thinking PTSD,
but you act out for others." Hannah told me.

She wanted to be a psychologist after that
class with Kimber.

I stared at her.

"Are you gonna kill me?" She asked.

"Why would I? You're innocent-- kinda.
Besides, I don't do that anymore." I said.

She giggled, "I'm not innocent, but I'll take
that compliment to heart, seeing as it's
coming from a serial killer superhero."

I'm retired.

And I was never a superhero.

Homicide Halloween

It was Halloween Week

Hannah got tickets to a horror carnival.

Katie-- I mean mom-- said I could go.

"No thanks," I said to Hannah.

I didn't go out much these days, I mostly just slept.

I mean I never really went out before...

"Not an option, we're all going. I even got tickets for Roselle, Harrison, Hannah, her boyfriend, Jake-- one for Max, and even one for Z-"

"We should go," Max blurted out.

Because Z was Zoey.

"Freaking hell..." I murmured.

When we got there, it was already looking pretty bad. Apparently, some people had died of heart attacks. Could just be rumors.

"Guys in here!" Zoey yelled.

So I should probably introduce Zoey.

She's another old friend who moved away and recently moved back.

She had a scarring childhood and extreme mental conditioning. Zoey was heavily abused as a child, physically, mentally, sexually, and emotionally. She took up Krav Maga, a martial art that is considered the power effective in the world, from her Uncle Krishiv to fend off bullies. She learned to work through pain through fighting, she claims at this point she ignores pain. She created a habit of working out until her body nearly gives out, because her father always had high expectations of her, psychologically damaging her and causing her to give herself high expectations.

Despite all of this, she keeps moving. Zoey came up with a quote. "If you can't keep up, you should just die." She rarely ever cries or feels pity for herself, she said her mom would hit her when she cried, so she developed a complex about crying due to fear of pain. When she gets "tired", she punches herself in the face to "wake herself up." Recently, she started saying one of my quotes "a ball has to hit the floor to bounce back up." However, her greatest motivation to keep moving is her friends.

At the end of the day, like everyone else, Zoey still has flaws. First off, she's afraid of death, I can't be sure or ask her for fear of setting her off, but I assume it may be due to her nearly being beaten to death at one point. Zoey can be triggered by abuse, any sort of abuse, sexual, physical, emotional, etc. She refused to stay away from the TV screen at one point, so now she needs glasses. She has trouble keeping a relationship, I'll spare you the details but she's been on and off with our friend Ken. Her body is filled with bruises and scars, even burns sometimes. I assume the bruises and scars are from fighting because she needs to make money, but no one seems to understand the burns.

She doesn't play much of a role in this book, but just like Max, she will in later books.

Spoilers-- at the time this book is set in. She'd kill me with ease.

Anyway, she was pointing at a building with a poorly drawn sign that said;

"GATEWAY TO HELL"

"Generic as hell..." I murmured.

It was pitch black inside. To the point that you'd think it was something supernatural, cloaking all the possible light.

Then something tapped Jake on the shoulder, to which he elbowed it in the neck.

It was a man. Probably in his early 20's, he was pale and scrawny.

"Damn reflexes...Sorry man. Are you okay?" Jake reached out a hand.

"I think I knocked him out," Jake said.

"...Jake, he's dead," Max said, trying to feel the man's pulse.

"What?!" Jake was mortified.

There was a dead man, probably only in his 20s, wearing a mask which was now half off his face.

"Is everything okay in there?" A voice called as the door opened.

"What did you do!?" A chubby middle-aged man, who seemed to be security yelled.

I kicked him in the face.

"Have you freaking lost it?" Roselle nearly yelled.

"Shut up, we have to destroy the body and make sure this guy doesn't say anything," I said.

"He's lost it..." Roselle complained.

I don't know if I ever had it.

We were at the end of the lot, no one else was there and we could escape through the back of the building. Just in case Harrison would use the mask while getting the bodies out, we were to follow later on, but in the meantime just act casual.

"Act casual? How the actual hell are we supposed to do that? This is murder and kidnapping. Shit, this is bad..." Roselle argued, pacing back and forth.

"Just follow my lead, we'll be fine," I said.

I don't know how but we made it out with two bodies.

I almost dropped the body several times due to the stab wound on my hand still healing.

I had a minor headache too, but whatever.

So I ignored it.

We had gone to my house and dumped the body in a tub filled with DM 1-971 in a basement under my basement.

Harrison showed the room to me.

The room was thirty feet underground with soundproof walls.

I decided I'd make it my Kill Lair…

I'll work on the name.

Couldn't hurt to make it bigger too.

After a few hours, the body was dissolved.

As for the security guard? Maybe it's better if I don't tell you what I did.

Think Batman intimidation, except I'm a serial killer.

"I guess we're all in this now…" Roselle murmured sleepily.

"You still awake Jake?" I asked, I was pretty awake.

"Ya." Jake was awake.

"I guess these idiots are staying the night. How about you?" I asked.

"My parents would kill me if I stayed with you guys after midnight," Jake said.

"Dude…" I nearly laughed.

"Ya?" Jake asked.

"It's five in the morning..." I chuckled.

"Shit," Jake said.

That night into that morning, I felt…

Alive.

The Carnival Killer

According to the news, there was a found body and a missing one.

I take credit for the latter.

I looked at Harrison.

"Wasn't me." He shrugged and pulled out a cigarette.

"Stop with the cancer sticks."

"I am a pimp who wants death!" He joked.

He wore a lot of purple these days.

Anyway, the head was torn off.

They called him The Carnival Killer.

That got me thinking.

"Harrison, how are you a serial killer? You don't have a vanta black suit or anything." I asked.

"Well, I'm careful, less impulsive than you. That's why my killings were always blamed on petty crimes. I'm stronger than you too. Francis and Jamie helped me out with the bodies. One night I called Jamie while she was allocated to me-- she picked me up and brought me to Francis, he helped me dissolve it. But if I had a serial killer name, I'd be... The Butcher Bastard."

"Harrison, our parents were married."

"It sounds cool though."

Harrison is three years younger than me...

Jamie died when I was 13...

This kid started killing people when he was a fucking child.

Is my family even human?

I turned my attention back to the TV

"The Carnival Killer huh...?"

"A girl came forward, saying the victim had been groping her earlier, and a tall man was just staring at it happening. The girl said it was too dark to see the tall man's face. Other witnesses place the man's height at about 6'9, although as attention was not focused on the man, identification is difficult, and a proper height is unquantifiable. In addition, he has left no evidence at the crime scene known to the public at the moment. A killer who killed a child molester and is giving the police a runaround. Is it possible we have a new-- and taller-- Karma Killer?" I switched it off.

I had a few suspects, Tattus Arkangelo, he's tall and too smart. Literally smokes weed to

173

nerf himself so he can talk to people in any capacity, it's said he once hacked into NASA with a calculator. He also has a strong sense of what's right and wrong. Also, he's an Arkangelo...

Mickey Milanoo, he's socially inept so he uses violence to cope. Incredibly religious, but carries around a Glock and a machete. Maybe he had a crush on the girl?

Karl Tylers is pretty tall now. Maybe he had a crush on the girl?

So is Luka Tonfa. Maybe he had a crush on-- oh wait he's gay.

But for Mickey and Karl and even Tattus, the crushing idea is kinda valid.

And, there was one more suspect.

And I hoped I was wrong.

But the Carnival Killer seems to be killing bad people, at least going by the one he's killed so far. Thinking back on it, I shouldn't have killed Monty, because Monty was the only person who really understood me, the only one I could have talked to.

If I hadn't killed Monty, maybe we'd be partners in crime and crime-fighting...

But being alone is good, it gives you time to see what there is to hate about yourself.

Me? I have people.

But they're just light sources.

I'll always be alone in the dark.

But at least I can see to a degree.

And with my limited vision, I decided something.

I'm gonna kill the Carnival Killer.

Blood Glue

"You don't own me! I can hang out with Mickey if I want!" Hannah yelled at Jake.

"You are such a bitch!" Jake yelled at his girlfriend.

"If I'm such a bitch maybe we should break up!" Hannah yelled louder.

9th-grade drama.

"Sure... Alana sucks me better anyway." Jake said.

I nearly killed Jake right then and there.

…

But we were in the school hallway...

"Kill him," Monty's ghost-- my hallucination-- said in my mind.

I punched Jake in the face.

My hand stung.

I clenched my teeth and hoped Jake would just give up so I wouldn't fuck up my hand more.

I could totally fight him, but I'd made progress in its healing, so I didn't want to open the wound again.

"Good enough for now," Monty said.

So I just stared at him, and he didn't swing back.

Hannah showed up at my house.

"Hey--" I started to say.

She threw herself into my arms, I caught her.

"Hannah?"

"Do you miss Kimber?"

"What?" It was a touchy subject.

"Does it hurt?"

"...Yeah, always will."

"Then maybe we can ease each other's pain...? Like that night before?"

What night?

I stopped her.

"You shouldn't use others as glue just to patch up a hole in your heart."

"Isn't that what you do when you murder people?"

"Go home, Hannah."

The Woman from Taured

Jake turned up dead.

Hannah was a suspect after someone told the cops that they broke up.

They had nothing to tie her to the crime, so they couldn't arrest her.

I saw the body.

Jake was tortured, his chest puffed up.

Then more bodies showed up.

Nude and mutilated, tortured, their chests puffed up.

Always on beds.

All of the men had erections, which is rare among the dead. Typically you'd lose it, erections happen when sponge-like tissue inside the penis fills up with blood. But, when you die blood doesn't naturally pump itself into the penis. So typically you'd lose it.

"I read that if you die face-down, your blood could possibly settle in your penis—which creates the appearance of a boner." Harrison walked into my room while I was doing research, he was drinking some orange juice.

"But the men were face-up-- wait, why do you know that?" I asked my brother while working with him.

"Death erections are a thing. Death by hanging has been observed to affect the genitals of men. A more or less complete state of erection of the penis is a frequent occurrence. The phenomenon has been attributed to pressure on the cerebellum created by a noose." He ignored my question and gave me another explanation.

"But why do you know that?" I asked again.

He smiled.

"You're not the only brainiac in our family," Harrison explained

"Fair enough-- there were no signs of hanging, no marks on the neck, no noose anywhere, none of it," I said.

"Spinal cord injuries are known to be associated with long-term erections. Injuries to the cerebellum or spinal cord are often associated with long-term erections in living patients." Harrison told me.

"There were no damages to the spinal cords, and they were dead," I informed my brother

"It can also be caused by fatal gunshots to the head, damage to major blood vessels, and violent death by poisoning. A long-term post mortem erection is an indicator that death was likely swift and violent." Harrison explained.

"There was no gunshot or violent sign of death, the torture was never what killed them. There were just always two wounds, a wound on their erection, and on their chests." I told him.

"Check the wounds, see what's in them." Harrison had a plan it seemed.

"How will I do that?"

"You're a billionaire, bribes aren't exactly taxing on your bank account."

In the wounds of the men were modified doses of Synthol, a substance bodybuilders use temporary implants. It's injected deeply into the muscle and immediately enlarges it.

The effects of Synthol can be fatal including permanent muscle disfigurement, muscle fibrosis, and the development of muscle ulcers and wounds.

This usually takes 4-5 years to hurt someone, but this was a custom version, the effects were done in a few hours.

My conclusion? Someone was capturing men-- likely with the promise of sex-- and then torturing them, and killing them with huge doses of modified Synthol.

Captured

I let her capture me.

I went to the nightclub many of the men were seen at.

I don't sleep much anymore... again.

Granted I did train myself to require a lot less sleep than most people.

But yeah, after a few near hookups, I found her.

I'm a virgin, don't worry.

I woke up tied up, again.

"Oh, you're awake." She greeted me.

"Yeah, I recommend you let me go," I said.

"And why's that?" She asked.

I got up.

"Cause I already cut the ropes," I said.

"What? How?" She stepped back, holding a knife in my direction.

"In my line of work, I had to learn how to escape things like ropes and chains."

Also, my hand had basically completely healed.

My eye was getting there.

"Who are you?" She asked another question.

"A serial killer," I said.

"Then you're like me!" She said,

"I kill, but it's to protect, I like helping people. Why did you kill those men? What did they do? Are they part of a trafficking ring or something? I can help you if you give me a good reason."

"I... do it to get off."

"So they're innocent?"

"Kill her." Monty was back.

"Innocent!? All these creatures just want sex! All men do!"

"I mean-- I'm a virgin."

"You're a good-looking kid-- what? You never loved anyone?"

"I did-- she hates me. I haven't moved on. Don't think I will. A girl actually came onto me the other day--"

"You have to live with the living, she'd want you to move on. Besides, you can die at any time just do what makes you feel good."

We were both silent for a moment.

I guess she was right

Kimber was scared of me, but Hannah accepts me.

I have the right to indulge in human pleasures.

"You're right... thank you-- Are you gonna stop torturing and killing men?"

"Yes." She said,

I let her go.

...

Then another body turned up, with the same symptoms.

She woke up in my second basement, thirty feet under my house.

You could call it a Batcave, but it's more of a Dexter Morgan Kill Room.

It heats up to evaporate blood.

It's also soundproof! Good thing too, my adoptive mom, Katie Myers, drops by the house often.

She'd been more protective of me and my brother Harrison since the Carnival Killer incident.

But yeah, this was my Killcave.

My victim understood immediately.

"Fuck you! No one will ever love you! You're a monster, you'll die alone and burn in hell! I hope your dick falls off and rots!"

"I'll see."

I placed my knife over her throat.

"I look forward to seeing you down there." I pressed down.

"Fucking finally." Monty showed up again.

"Will you get the fuck out of my head?"

"Maybe if you go to therapy."

"And tell them what? That I made a tulpa from a guy I murdered because he murdered someone I was going to murder?"

Monty shrugged.

Takes My Pain Away

I went to Hannah's house.

"Hey Karma--" She greeted me.

"Ease my pain," I said to her.

The rest of that night is a blur.

I remember her kissing me

Then she smiled in a way that told me I'd have to stop us from going too far.

And then we fell onto her couch.

I wonder where her parents were.

I got home around 3 in the morning.

"Karma!" I heard Katie Myers.

She owns my company until I turn 18, and she is my "mom."

These days she's more protective over Harrison and me, after the Carnival Killer incident.

"Yeah?" I asked.

"It is three in the morning, I was about to call search parties for you."

"For what reason?"

"You're 13."

"She's 14."

"What…? What!? What did you do Karma?"

"Don't worry about it, we just kissed, alot, sensually-- with tongue--"

Katie asked me a question without using words, as her mouth was agape… I didn't know if she had lost her ability to speak or if she had become a painting because she wasn't talking or moving.

"No Katie-- we didn't. We just kissed, socks on. Go home." I told her.

"You really have become rebellious, what happened to that sweet Karma that I knew?"

"Killed him in an alley, been dragging his body around town, pretending to be a warped version of him."

"What?"

"I'm a ghost. Go home, Kate," I said.

She did.

I had been on a downwards spiral lately, I knew that.

Well, I drank a lot.

I don't have an addictive personality.

Quite the opposite, in fact, I can literally stop anytime I want.

I've done it for random bursts of time.

But drinking isn't that bad, either I die of liver poisoning or I die in battle.

I wasn't a monster.

Okay, I am a monster-- but I don't beat people up when I'm drunk.

At least I wasn't smoking like Harrison, cigarettes burn my throat.

I could wash the burn with alcohol though...

Stamp of Approval on My Lips

I was hanging out with Hannah.

I noticed that since I spent that night with her-- Monty had shut up.

Which begs the question...

"So, do you approve?" I asked.

"Of what? That goofy shirt?" She asked, rolling a blunt.

She had gotten into weed, I didn't particularly like smoking cigarettes or weed, but I did the latter in company.

"Y'know... my habits," I told her.

"Oh, you mean your sexual deviancy?" She asked.

"I am not-- I mean my homicidal alter-ego," I said.

I had started thinking of The Karma Killer as less of a disguise, and more of an alternate version of myself.

"You only kill bad people right? The cops in this town and corrupt as fuck-- you're just helping them out. You're taking out the bad guys just like them-- Difference is you don't get a paycheck." She explained my life.

"I mean I literally have them on payroll." I pointed out.

"So you approve?" I asked.

"Take a hit, and I'll give you a stamp of approval."

"How does that--"

"I'm gonna kiss you dumbass."

"You are so bad at sexy talk." I laughed.

Dumb Bitch Cooper

I'm still looking for Carnival, but he covered his tracks well.

The winter snow helped cover his tracks I suppose.

I mean, I know exactly who he is. Jason Melandro.

He had a daughter.

But the guy completely disappeared from public record.

I think he killed his daughter too, she disappeared from public record as well.

So of course, he has to die next.

While I was doing research I got a call.

Hannah.

"Hey hun, what's--"

"Karma help." She said in a hushed tone.

I got up and sprinted to my door.

The call cut off.

I rushed out the house, not even getting my suit-- as if it would do anything, it's broad daylight. What? Would I change in the alley? Can't go around in my suit in the middle of the day.

I traced the signal.

It was a grocery store.

I didn't have my suit on.

I walked in anyway.

A man was holding the cashier at gunpoint.

He noticed me walking in.

He raised his gun at me.

I put on my best "scared face."

I raised my hands as if to say, "chill, I just got here, no idea what's going on!"

"Get on the ground!" The man said.

I started crouching.

I lay on the ground.

"Karma--" She said in a hushed tone before I put my finger to my lips.

"I want the secret stash too-- the one from my heist!" He went back to the cashier.

"What secret stash-- what heist?!" The cashier squeaked.

"Give it to me or I'll blow your brains out and find it myself--"

I pushed the aisle on the gunman.

He panicked and fired a shot.

Hannah flinched, and the cashier stumbled back. I just tore out my shoelace and wrapped it around the robber's neck while placing my foot on his gun arm.

I spun the man around until he could look at me.

I watched the life leave his eyes.

I watched his consciousness dissipate.

I watched everything he would ever do and ever do fade from reality.

He was dead.

I got up and walked to the cashier.

"You've seen my face, don't forget that I'll remember yours."

...

The cashier tattled on me.

He said The Karma Killer came out in broad daylight and killed the man.

Then The Karma Killer wiped the security cameras as he usually does.

I burned the shoelace.

And the shoe.

It was on the news.

The delusional idiot thought he was D.B. Cooper, and that the cashier was holding his money.

Another loon.

Do I belong on that list?

Tattus Arkangelo

So, I messed up.

I left the store without a disguise.

195

And Tattus Arkangelo has a photographic memory.

He approached me at school.

"Wanna tell me why you walked into a bodega, The Karma Killer killed someone, and then you walked out?"

"I do not want to tell you that."

"KK didn't even enter or leave that grocery store, you did."

"Secret tunnels? Also, The Karma Killer operates exclusively at night."

"You're lucky Hannah and I live in a shitty neighborhood-- if you were in your area-- people would be calling the police like a white kid got murdered."

"I mean he was white--" I started to say.

"And there's your name, Karma. You're clearly the Karma Killer."

Does he think the person who gave me that name knows my real name?

"Look, I recommend you let it go, he nearly killed my girlfriend-- I don't kill good people."

"Would you kill me?"

"You're tempting me."

"Just don't kill any innocents, and I won't destroy you. The second you step out of line? I'll break your fucking neck."

So that's what that feels like.

"I like you." I said.

She's Not Mine

Hannah called me.

It was getting a bit excessive lately, but she takes my mind off things, she makes me happy.

Besides, I genuinely like her, and she accepts me.

"Ryan Daisyfield is throwing a party tonight, you coming?"

I looked at my computer screen.

Homework took literally five minutes. I was looking at information about Carnival, and Jason Melandro.

I decided I needed a break.

"Yeah sure."

...

It was a cane party.

Of course, it was a cane party.

It was winter after all.

And the leftover powder could just be tossed into the snow.

People had to take off their heavy clothing which was needed for the winter, but no one dared steal from others for various reasons, one of the reasons being me.

Some older kids were snorting.

The younger kids were just drinking…

There's some attempt at rationality about how "anyone under 16 shouldn't do cocaine."

As if anyone over 16 should do it anyway.

I was younger than nearly everyone in the room, including previously mentioned younger kids.

I still drank.

Then I saw a guy with a hand on Hannah's shoulder.

"That's my girl--" I said.

"Bitch ain't got your name tatted." The boy said.

Alejandro Ronalds.

"She belongs to me."

"Karma--" Hannah tried to speak.

"Get off her." I got in Ale's face.

"You wanna die rich boy? You think just because you're rich and beefed up these last few months that you're Batman?"

"Batman would leave you alive," I said.

Hannah practically dragged me out of the house.

"What the fuck is your problem?!" She practically shrieked.

"He was touching my girl--"

"I don't belong to you!"

"I don't belong to anyone, I'm not an object!" She yelled.

"But you're my girl."

"But do I belong to you?" She tested me.

"..." I was quiet.

"..." She was quiet.

I decided to push her buttons.

"Yes." I failed.

With a smile on my face.

"Go fuck yourself Karma-- you're worse than Jake."

"Is that why he's dead?"

She seemed upset by that, "what the fuck is wrong with you? He was a dick-- but he was a human being."

"And now he's compost. It looks like you only attract sleazebags and assholes. Like that guy at the last party, we went to"

"What guy at the party?"

"The one where the guy felt you up, had you moaning."

Something clicked in her head.

She remembered something.

"Did you do anything about it?"

"... I dipped from the party."

"You… fucking asshole!" She ran away crying.

"Hannah--" I reached out to her--

She was gone.

"You fucked up." Monty was there again.

MOTHERFUCK.

She Hates Me

I fucked up, bad.

Even if I was drunk it wouldn't excuse it, that was heartless... at least bringing it up in the way I did.

She had a right to know, but I was just being a complete asswipe.

Hannah didn't talk to me after that night.

I guess she didn't snitch because I had saved her life during the D.B. Cooper incident, maybe she felt she owed me.

She also started using some unhealthy coping mechanisms for her sexual abuse.

And I feared she was using it to cope with knowing what I was.

From shooting up to nearly getting shot inside of.

And I just had to watch.

I realized that I kept killing people-- if I didn't kill them myself? They die seemingly for being close to me. And if they didn't die? They become fucked up or self-destructive-- because of what I am.

I knew the breakup wasn't the worst thing that could happen, I probably wasn't going to kill myself over it or anything-- this time, but it still sucked.

I was legitimately sad though.

I needed a kill.

I stayed up for four nights searching for clues on Carnival.

I hadn't even shaved in the last 3 days, my facial hair was itchy... I started early.

I ignored it.

I took some of my own questionable substances to stay awake.

And I drank a lot-- if I was going to hurt people because I drank, I might as well double down and ruin my life.

This just made me have to take more substances to stay awake.

I had the brain cells to spare though.

But I needed a good kill.

Then it was on the news "Jason Melandro identified as The Carnival Killer and arrested, police searching for his daughter."

The police had him.

I realized I wasn't in control of a lot of things.

My drinking.

My love life.

The mortality and morality of my friends and family.

Carnival.

The One That Got Away

I decided to settle.

I actually ran into him by mistake.

He was an old creep.

I actually passed out in an alley surrounded by snow.

I was a god fallen from heaven.

Well, a rich boy sleeping on the streets but close enough.

I saw him with a kid.

He had her against a wall.

"Get off her--" I tackled him sloppily, and we both fell into the snow.

"Who the fuck are you?" He asked, he was Russian

Dedushka.

It means grandpa in Russian.

"I'm a fucking asshole." Wait shit wrong line…

"You shoulda booked a flight back to Moscow," I said.

"What do you want? Drugs?" Somehow he was scared of me even though I was a mess and didn't even come up to his chest.

"Death is my drug."

"Who are you?!"

"Tired."

"If you tell on me-- I'll say you tried to kill me!"

"I am literally... a serial killer." I had to choke out.

"Then we--"

"We are not the same-- I can't kill a kid."

A rock smashed into Deduska's head.

I heard him.

"Karma, what the fuck are you doing?" Tattus asked me.

"Trying to fucking kill myself," I said.

"By fighting an old man?"

"Yes."

"You're a fucking mess Karma, you're not thinking straight."

"At least I am not straight-- wait shit-- at least I am straight!"

"I literally hooked up with Jesse Christenshin not even an hour ago. Your comebacks are shot. How drunk are you?"

"I should have severe alcohol poisoning honestly."

He walked towards me.

I got ready for a fight.

He ducked under me and--

Walked me to his car.

"C'mon, I gotchu man."

Tattus told the kid to run.

I woke up in an unfamiliar house.

It wasn't a mansion.

I saw Tattus.

"Why the fuck am I tied up?" I asked.

"Because you were trying to kill me last night after you knocked out on my bed."

"Please tell me we didn't sleep together."

Tattus cracked a smile, "Nah, I slept on the floor."

"Oh good, I didn't wanna downgrade that bad."

"Fuck you." Tattus chuckled, "When did you start making so many jokes anyway? Everyone at school notices it too."

"I dunno, maybe it's just coping with my life falling the fuck apart and it being my fault?"

"You're trying to ruin your own life?"

"Tattus, I am a fucking serial killer. I thought I accepted it, but no matter how clean the mirror is-- I see a monster."

"You are a monster."

"Thanks, Tati."

"But even the most disgusting creatures can do the right thing. You're doing the work for a system that's failing its people-- you're ending people who would normally just be locked away for years, and still hurt others even then."

"What are you saying?"

"Let's kill Carnival. Together... Except I don't physically kill him, you do that." He reached his hand out.

I shook it.

I'd kill Carnival.

But first I'd sleep.

This headache was fucking bad bro.

Bailed Out by The Guy Who's Gonna Bash Your Head In

I didn't actually pay bail.

It's difficult to pay with money for murder.

Believe me, I wish I could.

But several large bribes would suffice.

A few crowbar blows to the back of the head would suffice, but I wasn't in tip-top shape due to recovering from my bender.

Tattus could use a crowbar though, he didn't do enough substances to knock out an elephant yesterday.

Carnival woke up in my kill dungeon.

Still working on it...

"What is this place?" Carnival asked.

"Hell," I said.

He saw my black mask, and I saw Tattus' white mask, which was actually just a piece of paper that Tattus cut out and taped onto his face, but I digress.

I stared at Tattus in confusion.

"What?" Tattus asked.

"Why'd you do it?" I asked Carnival, ignoring Tattus.

"I wanted to help people," Carnival said.

"Bull-fucking-shit, you're using the Karma Killings as a cover for killing people," Tattus said.

"No-- I'm not!" Carnival yelled.

"You murdered your own daughter--" I said.

"Oh no, Casey-- where's Casey?!" Carnival panicked.

I looked at Tattus.

"I… did see a girl being questioned, and she did look a lot like him," Tattus said.

"You don't kill for pleasure?" I asked Carnival.

"I just felt bad for that girl-- she was being touched like I was when I was her age--" Carnival was freaking out.

"Karma," Tattus warned me.

"We're gonna find your daughter too--" I said.

"Please don't hurt her!" Jason begged.

"Stay here Tatts." I walked off.

Kidnapping a Kid

I skipped school to kidnap Jason's daughter.

She was in police custody, I guess drifters don't really go to school anyway.

We met up with Jason at a randevu point.

Her dad was wearing makeup to disguise himself. After all, he'd just been broken out of prison.

Speaking of which, The Karma Killer was now a hot topic again-- "he broke a murderer out of jail alongside another criminal-- why?"

Tattus called his vigilante persona, "The Totem."

Playing a seriously dangerous game with these names...

Anyway, we were going to the airport.

Casey was laughing as she held her dad's hand, ice cream from my fridge in her other hand. I thought it was weird that she wanted ice cream in the chilly weather, but I didn't say anything.

Then Jason fell to the floor.

I threw myself over, Suzy.

Tattus pulled out a BB gun.

There was a hole in the window behind Jason.

Someone sniped Jason.

He was dead.

"Oh fuck!" Monty said.

"Holy shit Monty shut the fuck up!"

"Or what?"

"Or I'll slit your throat again!"

Monty shut up.

No Looking Back

Suzy went into foster care.

It turns out her mother had killed herself a few years ago.

Her dad just wanted to go on a road trip with his daughter.

They took off.

They were in Darklind when Jason saw a girl being molested.

He couldn't help himself.

And I couldn't help his daughter.

I was angry.

My kills reflected that.

I had become brutal.

More brutal.

I stabbed this one guy 16 times one night.

I was losing it…

Speaking of my mental state, I thought of Hannah, and how she was good with the mind.

She wanted to be a psychologist.

214

I realized that Hannah saw how broken I was and still accepted me.

That's something I didn't get from Kimber, acceptance.

I went to talk to Hannah at a party.

She was kissing Mickey Milanoo.

Was I sad?

Maybe I was happy that she was happy? I don't think I cared that she was angry at me.

I don't feel things like I used to, I don't feel the warmth of the candles on my skin anymore.

I can barely see in the dark, and it doesn't bother me.

Oh well.

Everyone dies. In the end, their struggles are just consumed by the darkness, and never seen again. I don't need lights, I'm used to the dark.

Which is good, because the world seems to be getting darker.

And if I can't save the world-- if it becomes consumed by darkness-- I'll probably just end up taking it over, or destroying it.

For now? I'd find Jason's killer, who I am now convinced was Val's killer, because of the circumstances surrounding Jason's killer.

Cameras were wiped, bullets unregistered, and no one in the area has bought a sniper as of late-- the first of those being the reason that I couldn't be documented as being associated with them.

I mean I could have done that anyway.

But the cameras being wiped also means I couldn't see who it was.

This guy took two of my big bads…Now whoever did, is my big bad.

The title of The Perfect Killer can only belong to one person… He has it right now, because not even I have caught him.

But I'll own the belt of victory…

And I'll choke the previous owner with the strap.

Because the only true justice for people like that is a violent, painful death.

But, remember that I'm a killer too.

And I can't go back.